COW

C000186818

His Ranch. His R

MAGGIE CARPENTER
Cover Image
ROB LANG
https://www.roblangimages.com
Cover: ShanoffDesigns.com
Published by: Dark Secrets Press
Visit Maggie Carpenter
http://www.MaggieCarpenter.com
https://www.facebook.com/MaggieCarpenterWriter
https://twitter.com/magcarpenter2

PROLOGUE

Turning her 1934 renovated Ford pickup off the country road, Carly Kincaid drove down the wide lane towards the imposing wrought iron gates. Two huge stone horse heads atop the tall pillars at either side, their mouths open and their eyes wide, stared down at her as she pulled to a stop and lowered her window. Pushing the only button on the call box, she felt a flurry of nerves. Working on a small ranch in the middle of nowhere may not be everyone's cup of tea, but it was her dream job.

"Yes?"

"Hi, it's Carly Kincaid."

"Drive up to the house, park next to the truck and come to the front door."

"Thank you."

The massive gates swung open, and moving up a gentle slope, the single story home came into view. It was a picture book log cabin, except it wasn't a cabin. The sprawling home on the knoll was surrounded by manicured gardens, and she imagined the view overlooking the sprawling ranch below would be spectacular. Drawing closer she could see the portico, then she spotted the gleaming late model black truck to the side of the garage in what appeared to be a parking area. Rolling to a stop next to it and climbing from her eye-catching automobile, she was met by a surprisingly cold breeze. Grabbing her leather satchel she walked swiftly to the front door, but before she had time to ring the bell, it opened. An attractive middle-aged woman smiled a greeting.

"Good afternoon, please come in."

Walking inside, Carly glanced around the large foyer and into the room beyond. Cowhide rugs sat on a dark tile floor, paintings of western scenes hung on the walls, and a life-sized antique wooden indian with a full feathered headdress was standing against the step-down entrance into the lounge.

"Wait here, please."

2

Carly commanded her heart to stop hammering. Her resume had landed her the interview, and she didn't want to blow it by being a nervous wreck.

"Mr. Parker will see you now."

Looking down the wide hallway, she could see the woman waiting with her arm gesturing towards an arched doorway. Hurrying forward, Carly smiled at her, then walked into an impressive office.

The man behind the desk was reading, but she could see his wide shoulders and powerful muscles beneath the rolled up shirt sleeves. Hearing the door close behind her, she paused, not sure if she should sit down or wait to be invited, but he suddenly raised his head.

She caught her breath.

He was the most gorgeous man she'd ever seen.

His eyes were smoky brown, his lips amazingly full, and his handsome features would make any male model envious.

"Carly Kincaid, I'm Keith Parker. Have a seat."

His voice matched his drop-dead good looks. It was deep and husky, and she was grateful for the invitation to sit down. Her knees were weak.

"Tell me why I should hire you?"

The abrupt, unexpected question took her by surprise, as did the answer that unexpectedly sprang from her lips.

"Because you won't find anyone better."

Breaking into a broad grin, he leaned across the desk.

"How could you possibly know that?"

"That's a better question. Sorry, that sounded rude. I didn't mean it to be."

"Don't apologize, I like your moxie, and you're right, my second question was better. Do you have an answer?"

"I do. Mr. Parker, for me, it's all about the horse. If I'm tired but the horse needs something, my break has to wait. If there's an unexpected blast of icy rain or snow and I don't think the blanket is warm enough

I'll trudge through the weather to change it. You may find a better rider, or a person with more experience, but you'll be hard-pressed to find anyone more dedicated to a horse's welfare than I am."

"That's about the finest response to an interview question I think I've ever heard," he remarked, nodding his head, "and I can tell you meant every word."

"Thank you. I did."

"You do realize there's nothin' much to do around here after the barn door is closed. The town's small, no nightlife to speak of, though I hear folks gather in the diner or the tavern down near the river. You sure you're not gonna get bored?"

"If I wanted a nightlife I wouldn't be looking to get away from the city. All I want is to be around horses in an environment that suits them, and by that I mean wide open spaces, owners who care about them, who call a vet out when—"

"You can stop right there," he declared, holding up his hand. "That's exactly the kinda attitude I've been lookin' for."

"I'm so pleased to hear that. When I read through the information packet you sent me explaining how you feed, and outlining the training schedule, I thought it sounded great."

"You gotta horse of your own?"

"Winston. He's a big, grey warmblood. He's a retired show horse and he's a dream. I ride him in a halter."

"I'll just bet you do," he murmured, tilting his head to the side. "Sandy, that's the girl who's leavin', she's a lot like you. She's been here two years and I'll be sorry to see her go."

"May I ask why she's leaving?"

"She's gone and got herself pregnant. She'll be hitched in a month or so."

"To someone local?"

"Yep. Carly, I think you're just the person to take over for her, but I'd like you to stay here for a couple of days and make sure this is what you think it is. I also need to see if we click, and there's also Andy, my manager and trainer. If things work out you'll be livin' in a cabin near the barn. Sandy's already moved in with her fiancé, so you can try it on for size."

"Staying for a couple of days is an excellent idea. Thanks for the opportunity."

"How far did you drive to get here?"

"About three hours."

"Three hours. That's not next door. Here's what I'm gonna do. I'll have Elsie bring you some coffee and somethin' to eat, and I want you to sit in the livin' room by the fire and read through a detailed description of the job. Even more important is my list of rules. There's no sense you drivin' all the way home and all the way back here without knowin' what's expected."

"That sounds good. Thank you, I'd like that very much."

"There's no rush. Elsie will check on you from time to time, and when you're ready she'll bring you back here. Any questions?"

"How many horses do you have, and what's the turnaround like?"

"Never have more than ten. When one sells, I'm never in a hurry for the next one, but it usually happens pretty quick."

"I noticed the size of your stalls. I can understand why you'd have to limit the number."

"Horses need to move around, but I don't like them out in bad conditions. If they have to be stuck inside because of a blizzard they need space. Why don't people understand that?"

"I know, right?" she exclaimed. "That's another reason I had to get out of the city. Everyone has their horse locked in a stall and they think it's okay. Drives me crazy. Stall is just a fancy name for cage, at least it is in my book."

"You and I are on the same page about that," he said firmly, opening a desk drawer and withdrawing a folder. "Here you go. If you have any concerns make sure you voice them. We'll either work them out or we won't."

"Thank you," she said, rising to her feet and accepting the folder.

"What do you have in that satchel?"

"Photographs, some references, and DVD's of me riding. I know I sent you some, but I thought I'd bring more in case."

"Leave them here. I'll take a look."

Opening the worn leather bag, she pulled out a bulky envelope and placed it on his desk.

"Go to that front room off the foyer. Elsie will see you there."

"Thank you, Mr. Parker."

"May as well start callin' me Keith."

"Thank you, Keith," she said with a smile, and as she turned and left his office, an unexpected thought flashed through her head. Keith and Carly. The names had a nice ring to them.

Delighted by the turn of events, she walked down the hallway and into the inviting living room. A grouping of easy chairs in front of a natural rock fireplace beckoned, and she settled into the one nearest a wooden slab coffee table. Opening the folder, she found more pages than she'd expected, and decided to start with the job description. It was only a few minutes later the woman who had greeted her at the door walked in. Carrying a tray offering a thermos labeled Coffee, a small jug of cream, sugar, a sandwich and a few cakes, she set it down on the table.

"I wasn't sure what you'd like, but I made fresh tuna salad this morning. I promise there's very little mayonnaise."

"Thank you. I love tuna sandwiches."

"Keith said you'd driven three hours to get here. I figured you might have a bit of an appetite."

"This is so kind," Carly said, genuinely surprised. "I've been on a few job interviews, but never one like this."

"We're pretty close-knit in this place, and we take care of each other. I'll be back to check on you in a little while."

It had been an interesting comment, but not giving it a great deal of thought, and surrendering to her hunger pangs, Carly devoured the sandwich and downed two cups of coffee before returning to the paperwork.

The job description was precisely what she'd thought it would be, and she moved on to the rules. No smoking on the ranch anywhere at any time was good news. No alcohol consumption during working hours. There were various instructions about blanket care, grooming supplies and general barn guidelines, and a vague mention of disciplinary actions for breaking the rules, but the last rule was completely unexpected.

No details of the ranch or the ranch employees to be discussed outside the property. Any deviation from this rule will result in immediate termination.

There was one more document. A confidentiality agreement.

She'd had to sign one and send it in before she'd been granted the interview. This was a second one, and in complicated legal language, it reiterated that no employee could relay any information about the barn, its owner or workers, to a third party at any time for any reason either during or after employment. Any breach of contract would result in legal action. Carly had no problem respecting the man's privacy, but it did seem extreme.

"How are you doing?" Elsie asked, walking into the room and interrupting her thoughts.

"Fine, thanks. I just finished. I'm ready to see him, if he's ready for me."

"I'll ask. Would you like more coffee, or can I take this away?"

"That was delicious, thank you."

"Good, I'm glad. I'll only be a moment."

Rising to her feet, Carly ambled across the room to gaze out the window. As she watched the horses in their paddocks, some playing, some quietly grazing, she didn't care why the man was so secretive about himself and his ranch. This was where she wanted to work.

"You can go in."

Turning around, she found Elsie smiling at her. The woman seemed happy, and Carly flashed back to the earlier comment. *We're pretty close-knit in this place, and we take care of each other.* Now Carly understood. This wasn't a city stable with people coming and going and workers changing every few weeks. It was a small, elite operation, and everyone lived on the property.

Picking up the folder and her satchel, she left the comfortable living room and headed down the hall to the arched door which was now closed. She stood for a moment to take a breath, then knocked.

"Come in."

Pushing it open, she walked in, closed it behind her, and moved quickly across to the desk. Her pulse ticking up, she sat down and looked across at the compelling cowboy who could be her new boss.

"Your videos were great—just like the ones you sent."

"Thank you."

"So, any thoughts?"

"I don't have a problem with anything I read—though—I'm curious about why you like to keep the ranch so...what's the word...?"

"The word is confidential, and whether you take the job or not, before you leave here you'll have to sign that confidentiality agreement. I can't stress this enough. If you end up workin' here, you'll be goin' into town, and folks will ask you questions about me, about the horses, whatever, and you can't tell them a thing. Not one word. It might spike their curiosity a bit, but what goes on here is no-one's business. We don't advertise our horses. There's a handful of trainers and owners we supply, and that's it. I only speak to people on the phone when I'm negotiatin' price. I'm not interested in all the bullshit talk. I leave that to

Andy. He's my manager and handles all the PR and sales. Can I be any clearer?"

"I get it. Everything is confidential. I won't breathe a word."

"Good. Now there's one other matter. Like everything else, what I'm about to tell you doesn't leave this office. Understood?"

"Of course."

"If you step outside the rules, I will exact a punishment."

"Okay."

"I haven't told you what it is yet."

"Surely it would depend on the rule I broke, though I can't imagine I'll be making it a habit."

"Corporal discipline."

"What?" she gasped, looking at him wide-eyed. "You can't be serious."

"I know it's considered old-fashioned, but I'm an old-fashioned guy, and don't start squawkin' about abuse. What I'm talkin' about is nothin' like that. A few good swats on the ass never did anyone any harm, and the method gets results."

Carly could feel her face flush a deep red, and an odd feeling rolled through her stomach.

"If you've got a problem with that, no worries, I understand. You and I can part company with no hard feelin's."

"I, uh, I don't know what to say."

"If you don't break the rules, you don't have to worry about it."

"I guess that's true," she murmured. "How hard could it be?"

"Not hard at all. You keep to your own business, follow the posted signs, and don't go askin' a lotta questions. Do that, and you won't have a problem. See how it works? Just chewin' on the idea is an incentive to follow the rules."

"I suppose you're right, but this is completely unexpected. I'm not sure how I feel about it."

"Why don't you go home and give it some thought?"

Carly paused.

She wanted the job, and she could think of worse things than having the sexy cowboy smack her ass. As a few silent seconds ticked by, the thought sent an unexpected wash of moisture through her sex.

"I don't need to go home," she declared. "If you want me, I'd love to work here."

CHAPTER ONE
Three Weeks Later

Rolling her sparkling antique pickup to a stop under the carport, Carly climbed out and stepped on the porch of the modest cabin. It was her new home and she was thrilled. Sandy had promised to meet her there, but when no-one answered when she knocked, she pushed down the handle and opened the door. She wasn't surprised it was unlocked. The security on the ranch was unlike anything she'd ever seen, but it was understandable. There were some very expensive horses on the property.

Stepping into the small but comfortable cottage, she ambled through the cozy living room. Though there was central heating and air-conditioning, it also offered a gas fireplace with decorative logs. The kitchen boasted modern appliances, with a breakfast nook and bar stools at the counter. She loved everything about it, and after the jarring noise of the city, the peace and quiet was a slice of heaven. Moving into the bedroom, she was surprised to find the bed had been turned down exposing crisp white sheets.

"This is like being in a hotel," she mumbled, then spying a note sitting on the nightstand with her name scrawled across the envelope, she picked it up and pulled out the folded paper.

Carly,

We're delighted to have you at Dream Horse Ranch. If you need anything or have any questions please don't hesitate to ask. Keith would like you to join us for dinner at the house this evening to officially welcome you. Andy and Salvo will also be there. Any time around seven o'clock will be fine, and we dress casually, so don't worry about what to wear.

Warmly, Elsie.

Carly sat on the edge of the bed and let out a breath. Dream Horse Ranch was indeed a dream come true. It was a small facility with beautiful horses, and reading the note a second time, she had to smile.

Salvo, the stable hand, was a big, burly, Italian, but he was young. She'd guessed him to be around twenty, and he'd been surprisingly shy when Sandy had made the introductions.

Andy, the trainer and manager, she had yet to meet. He'd unexpectedly been called away during the two days she'd stayed there, and she was still surprised Keith had hired her without Andy's approval. Though it was slightly unnerving, she had faith that Keith was confident the two of them would get along.

"Hello? Carly? Are you here?" a voice called from the living room.

"Hi, Sandy, thanks for being here," Carly called back, hurrying from the bedroom to meet her.

"It's my pleasure. Being back here is nice," Sandy said with a sigh. "I'm already missing it."

"Are you sorry to be leaving? Surely you must be excited about having your baby and getting married."

"Both. I loved my job and I'll miss the horses, but I love Mark more, and I know I'm doing the right thing."

"I wish you could help me through the first few days," Carly remarked. "Jumping in like this is a bit nerve-racking."

"You have my number. Call me any time," Sandy said reassuringly, "but you don't have to worry. You're a terrific rider. You'll do great. Oh, before I forget, the oven cooks hot."

"Ah, thanks. Good to know. I do like to bake occasionally, especially when the weather turns cold."

"If you need any pots or dishes, ask Elsie. Her kitchen is ridiculous. She's a gourmet cook, and she has more stuff than a cafeteria, but if she doesn't have what you need she'll get it for you. She's in charge of domestic supplies."

"What about Keith?" Carly asked tentatively. "Any advice there?"

Sandy paused.

"Uh...I'm not sure how to answer that."

"Sorry, I didn't mean to put you on the spot," Carly said hastily. "I just meant, does he have any quirks I should know about?"

"You didn't put me on the spot. The thing is, he's a very attractive guy."

"I hadn't noticed," Carly quipped with a grin, "but I don't see that as a problem."

"You might."

"What do you mean?"

"Falling for him is easy. I did, I had a terrible crush on him when I first started, but he never showed any interest in me. I'm glad now. Mark is amazing."

"I can't believe someone like Keith doesn't have a girlfriend," Carly remarked thoughtfully. "Or does he?"

"In the two years I've been here, I've never seen him with a woman, but he goes away a lot."

"He does? How often?"

"Sometimes he'll be gone a few days, sometimes a week."

"Where does he go?"

"I have no idea."

"Huh. That's curious."

"Don't bother trying to find out, you won't. He never talks about himself, and I strongly advise not to ask. He's really touchy when it comes to details about his life outside this place. He's kind, but he can be just as tough. If he says no, he means it."

"Sandy, can I ask you something?"

"Sure."

"The corporal punishment thing. Don't you think that's a bit weird? Did he ever...?"

"Oh, that! Yeah," she said with a nod, then threw back her head and laughed. "When I started I thought it was weird too, but that didn't last long. Try sexy as hell."

Carly began giggling.

"I thought it might be. Do you think he gets off on spanking?"

"Maybe, I don't know. What he did to me was quick. I guess you could say clinical. Quick and clinical, but as far as I was concerned, the whole thing was sexy as hell."

"How often?" Carly asked, becoming intrigued and tantalized by the story.

"Twice."

"Did the other guys know?"

"Absolutely not!" Sandy said vehemently. "Keith was absolutely clear about that. He didn't want me embarrassed."

"What was your crime?"

"My first mistake was on purpose," Sandy replied, lowering her voice. "I couldn't help it. I just had to see what he'd do."

"That's funny. I'm thinking along those lines right now. Did he know?"

"I think he guessed, but he didn't say anything."

"So? Your crime? Or rather, crimes?"

"As you know, we start at eight o'clock, and that's eight o'clock sharp. You can see the front door from this cabin. I was supposed to meet him there one morning. When I saw him leave, I kept him waiting about ten minutes. He was pissed when I finally walked in, and he told me to meet him in his office when I finished work."

"Oh, my gosh. Were you scared?"

"Every single minute until it was time to go, but I was excited too. Does that sound weird?"

"Not at all. That's how I'd feel. What happened? Tell me everything. Every single detail."

"He scolded me, told me to put my hands on his desk, then he swatted me ten times with his hand. A smack for every minute I was late."

"Oh, my gosh. Over your jeans?"

"Yeah, but it still hurt. I think my face was redder than my ass though."

"This is so bizarre."

"I know, right?"

"And the other crime?"

"I have a bad habit of not screwing lids on tightly. He reminded me a couple of times, but one afternoon he knocked over a can of Venice Turpentine I'd just used. It spilled all over the barn aisle floor. He was furious."

"No! Venice Turpentine? That stuff is the stickiest, gooiest crap on the planet. I don't blame him for being pissed."

"He grabbed a crop and landed it a few times. That hurt like hell. Mind you, it broke the habit. I've screwed lids on tight ever since."

"I'm sure," Carly exclaimed, her eyes wide. "Call me crazy, but I want to pluck up the courage and put him to the test. Just thinking about it makes me feel...uh..."

"Hard to describe, isn't it?" Sandy said with wink.

"More like impossible."

"Let's wander down to the barn, see if you have any last minute questions."

"Great idea. I haven't met Andy yet. What's he like?"

"He's a bit reserved, easy going though," Sandy remarked as they left the cabin. "Totally unflappable."

"Has he been here long?"

"He and Keith go back a long way."

"I sure would like to know more about him," Carly said with a sigh. "Keith, I mean. Why is he so secretive?"

"Lord knows, but you won't find out a thing. Google him, and there's nothing there. Look up Dream Horse Ranch, and you'll see one page. A corporation with names, but no Keith Parker."

"That's impossible. No-one can be invisible, not with the internet. Ten years ago maybe, but privacy is a thing of the past."

"Obviously whoever Keith Parker is, he doesn't want to be found," Sandy whispered. "I decided it wasn't worth my time to go digging. There was no upside. If he found out, he'd fire me, and I'd probably just waste a whole lot of time and not find anything anyway."

"I wonder what the deal is."

"He's a decent guy, so he must have a good reason for wanting to stay under the radar."

"It does make you wonder though," Carly said thoughtfully. "Speak of the devil, isn't that him in front of the barn?"

"Sure is. He's not usually around this time of day. Maybe he saw you drive in."

As he raised his head to look across at them, Carly felt the butterflies in her stomach suddenly spring to life. His cream shirt was wide open, exposing his washboard stomach.

"Hey there," he said with a smile as they approached. "How are you, Carly? When is your horse arrivin'?"

"The trailer should be here in about thirty-minutes. I wanted to get here early so I could make sure everything was ready for him."

"Where's all your tack? Do you have a trunk?"

"My stuff is in my pickup. I wasn't sure where to park to unload it."

"Let's go inside and check out your stall," he said, turning to walk into the barn. "Winston's stall should be clean and full of fresh shavings, and Salvo put down plenty of rock pebbles in the corral behind it. The rainy season will hit soon. A big horse can stomp it down pretty quick."

"Thanks, Keith. I appreciate that, and so will Winston."

"Sandy, are you and Mark settled in?" Keith asked. "How is everything goin'?"

"We are, and I love our little house."

"You know you can come and visit whenever you want. If you need to go for a gallop up the hill, just let me know."

"I'll take you up on that."

"Yep, looks good," Keith remarked as they reached the large stall. "You'll have locker seven in that tack room," he continued, pointing across the aisle. "There should be plenty of space for your trunk, but why don't you go in and make sure?"

"Thanks, Keith," Carly replied, staring into his mesmerizing eyes.

"When you've got that squared away, go ahead and bring up your truck. I'll help you. Salvo's over at the hay barn."

"You don't mind?" Carly asked, surprised the boss would do such a thing.

"Of course not. I'll meet you in front of the barn in ten minutes. I need to make a call."

She watched him saunter away, then followed Sandy into the tack room.

"Carly, he likes you."

"He does?"

"Hell, yeah. Normally he'd text Salvo to come back, not offer to help you himself."

"Seriously?"

"That's not the only thing. Andy's the one who would normally tell you about the load of rock pebbles in your corral and where to put your stuff."

"Are you sure? Don't you think Keith just wants me to feel welcome."

"You believe what you want, but I know him. He's going out of his way for you."

"Wow. That's so cool."

"Be careful," Sandy warned, lowering her voice. "As much as I like him, we both know a guy like that could break your heart. Here, this will be yours."

As Sandy showed her the locker, Carly wondered if Sandy was right. Was the gorgeous cowboy really making an extra effort?

"You're a million miles away," Sandy remarked.

"Sorry. I just can't believe how lucky I am, but I should run down and get my truck."

"I'll come with you. I need to head home. Remember, if you have any questions about anything, just call me."

"That's great. Thanks."

"I wish there was enough work here for the two of us," Sandy remarked as they started down the barn aisle. "We'd be a good team."

"I agree, but you'll be busy with your baby soon."

"True."

Walking outside, they spotted Keith looking sexy as hell leaning against the trunk of a huge oak tree. He had a phone to his ear, and the wind was flapping his loose shirt.

"He looks like he's posing for a picture," Carly said with a sigh. "How did a guy like that, end up living in the middle of nowhere on a ranch like this, with no wife or girlfriend?"

"No clue," Sandy murmured, "and those are all good questions."

"Come to think of it, does he own this place, or just run it for someone else?"

"Another good question."

"Keith Parker. The mystery cowboy. All this is making him even more interesting."

"Interesting?" Sandy retorted with a giggle. "I don't think that's the word you were thinking."

"You might be right about that, but like you said, he'd break my heart. Nope, he's hands off. I'll definitely be keeping my distance." Then breaking into a sassy grin and shooting Sandy a wink, she added, "I'd better get my truck up here. I don't want to keep him waiting."

"Very funny, but are you sure about that?"

"I plead the fifth!" Carly said with a giggle.

CHAPTER TWO

Driving her truck up the gentle slope towards the barn, Carly noticed Keith was no longer on the phone and leaning against the tree, but was waiting for her in front of the barn. As she rolled to a stop, he stepped forward and opened her door.

"This is quite a vehicle," he exclaimed, eyeing the unique pickup.

"She's my pride and joy, except for Winston of course. I call her Daisy," Carly replied, climbing out and smiling up at him.

He smiled back, but to her horror she felt her face flush red, and moving quickly around to the back, she lowered the tailgate.

"Salvo's on his way," he remarked, hoisting her saddle up and over the side. "I figured your tack trunk would take the two of us."

"It probably will," she said, glancing at him and admiring his ripped physique. "My life is in there, or should I say my horse life. Let me grab my bridle bag and I'll walk in with you. Why does riding have to be such a stuff sport?"

"Good question," he said with a chuckle as they headed into the barn. "Saddles, halters, saddle pads, bits, blankets, coolers...the list goes on and on."

"No kidding, though I don't have any bits. I ride Winston in a halter."

"I saw that on your videos. Very impressive."

"Not really. People rely too much on equipment. I think most horses will do whatever you want once you've bonded with them and they trust you."

"That's a nice way to think. I've ridden in a rope halter a few times, but not leather like you do."

"Maybe you should take a leap of faith and give it a try. I assume you do have your own horse."

"Yep, Pinocchio."

"What a cute name. If you want to give it a shot, let me know. I'd love to watch."

"Maybe I will. Okay, here we are," he declared as they walked into the tack room. "You know the rules about keepin' the tack clean. Just wipe it all down at the end of the day, and that includes your own."

"That's already a habit," she assured him, taking her halters from the bag and hanging them up. "I think the two of us can manage the tack trunk if you don't want to wait for Salvo."

"Carly! Did you forget that rule already?"

"Uh..."

"The heavy liftin' is done by Andy, Salvo, or me. Bags of feed, trunks, whatever, that's not your job. If you hurt your back I've lost my rider."

"I remember," she said sheepishly. "I just thought—"

"Those are three dangerous words," he declared, staring down at her with a slight frown. "When someone says, *I just thought,* it usually means they didn't. Either that, or they decided to do somethin' they shouldn't."

Suddenly tongue-tied, she was searching for a response when Salvo appeared in the doorway.

"I'm here, boss. Hi, Carly," he said cheerily. "What do you need?"

"Carly's tack trunk," Keith answered, moving past her into the barn aisle. "You probably saw it in her pickup out front."

"That's a really cool truck, Carly," Salvo declared, turning to follow Keith outside. "You'll have to tell me about it when we get a minute."

"I'll be happy to," she called after him, then shook her head as she stared at the equipment surrounding her. "I should have taken up skiing. All I'd have to worry about is boots, poles and skis."

Moving to the window, she watched Keith and Salvo lift her trunk and carry it from her pickup. But Carly couldn't pull her eyes away from her new boss. She was drawn to everything about him. His dimples when he grinned, his confidence and take charge manner, the way he walked—

"This is ridiculous," she muttered, moving back to her locker. "I have to stop daydreaming about him. It could ruin everything, even if it is just in my head."

"Carly, there was no stand in your truck," Keith declared as he and Salvo carried her trunk carefully through the door. "Do you have one?"

"No, I don't. It disappeared during one of my moves."

"There are a couple in the supply room," Salvo piped up. "I'll be right back."

"Thank you," Carly said as Keith and Salvo placed the trunk on the floor. "It helps to have it elevated."

"No problem. We have plenty of everything around here."

"Keith, your ranch is beautiful," Carly remarked as Salvo hurried away. "How did you come up with the name?"

He tilted his head to the side and narrowed his eyes. For a moment Carly thought she'd made a mistake, but a moment later, he broke into a smile.

"The clients who come here are looking for the horse of their dreams. That's what we sell them."

"That's brilliant, but aren't your clients repeat customers?"

"Most are, but they have relatives and friends. As you probably gathered, you can't buy a horse here unless you're referred. I like to know where my horses are goin', and I don't like strangers here."

"So—this is your ranch? I wasn't sure."

His smile suddenly fell away, and she grit her teeth, silently cursing herself for asking the question.

"Here you go," Salvo declared, breaking the awkward moment as he walked in with the stand. "That should work."

As Salvo put it in place, then helped Keith lift the trunk, her phone vibrated. Pulling it from her back pocket and opening the text, she learned the horse trailer carrying her precious cargo was approaching the ranch.

"Winston will be here any minute!"

"That's great," Keith said, moving for the door, "but I'll have to meet him later. I need to be in my office for a call that's coming in. Let Salvo or Andy know if you need anything, and speaking of Andy, he'll show up as soon as Elsie alerts him the trailer is at the gate."

"Okay. Thanks for the help," she said, disappointed that he had to go.

"You're welcome."

Her heart still sinking as she watched him stride away, she silently scolded herself for asking about the ranch, and swore she wouldn't make such a stupid mistake again.

"You should move your pickup," Salvo said, breaking into her thoughts. "The trailer needs the turnaround area."

"Shoot, of course. I'll do it right now."

She hurried through the barn, but walking outside she paused to look up at the house on the knoll. Keith had left the golf cart and was moving quickly through the front door. Watching him, she had the strangest feeling he had left because he didn't want to be seen.

"If I'm right, that's really weird," she muttered. "What the hell is going on with you?"

Trying to push the question from her thoughts and heading towards her truck, she noticed a cowboy striding up from the paddocks. As he raised his hand in a wave, she realized he had to be Andy. The man was solidly built with a tanned, weathered face, and it suddenly struck her that Keith didn't have the complexion of an outdoorsman.

"Howdy, I'm guessin' you must be Carly," Andy said warmly as he approached. "I reckon you know I'm Andy. I'm lookin' forward to workin' with you."

"It's great to meet you," Carly replied, shaking his hand. "Sandy says you speak horse."

"I don't know about that," he said with a chuckle, "but we seem to get along pretty well. I can honestly say I never met a horse I didn't like. Carly, I've gotta tell you, I really enjoyed your videos. You've got a real easy way about your ridin'. Sorry I wasn't here when you stayed those two days."

"I appreciate the approval without meeting me."

"I trust Keith's instincts. His A-okay is good enough for me. I understand your boy's about to arrive."

"He is. I'm so excited, and I'm really happy to be here."

"This is a good barn. We're a team. We follow the rules and help each other. That's what keeps things runnin' smoothly."

He'd made a point of mentioning the rules, and she made a mental note to go back through them again when she returned to her cabin. Apparently they were a very big deal at Dream Horse Ranch, and not just to Keith.

"I'd like to talk some more, but I need to move my pickup."

"She's somethin'. I'd like to hear how you found a classic like that in such great condition."

"I'll be happy to tell you," she said, grinning as she climbed in. "Her name is Daisy. I'll be right back."

Though she couldn't wait to see her horse, as she drove down to her cabin, she couldn't stop thinking what an enigmatic figure Keith was. As she rolled beneath the carport, she turned off the engine and stared out the window.

"What if he's a wanted felon or something?" she mused. "No, I'm only thinking that way because dad's a criminal defense lawyer. Not everyone who likes privacy has nefarious reasons, and why am I torturing myself like this? I've only been here two minutes and I've already fallen in crush and decided the guy's an axe murderer. Good grief, girl, get a grip."

Determined to keep herself in check, she climbed from her truck and jogged back to the barn, arriving just as the trailer appeared in the driveway. Moving slowly into the open area where she'd been parked, it came to a slow stop. As she ran up to meet her longtime horse hauler, Paul Jackson, he stepped from the cab, looked around, then let out a whistle.

"Damn, girl, you sure landed on your feet. This place is ridiculous."

"Isn't it? And the horses are amazing."

"I can't believe you found this job from some little ad in a magazine?"

"I know. I almost went right past it."

"I'm surprised a place like this would have to advertise. Usually the high-end barns like this find their people through word-of-mouth. Those are some nice lookin' horses," he continued, staring out at the paddocks. "I could get this place some sales if you wanna connect us."

Not sure what to say, and seeing Andy striding towards them, she decided to let him answer Paul's question.

"That's the guy to talk to. I just got here. I have no idea how this place runs. Can we please get Winston out now?"

"Yeah, yeah, sure, sorry. I just didn't expect anything like this."

Following him to the back of the trailer, she stood impatiently as he opened the doors, then seeing her big grey gelding she broke into a broad grin.

"Hey big fella," she said as the horse turned its head. "Sure is good to see you."

Paul began backing him out, and as Winston stepped down the ramp, Carly took the lead rope. He sniffed the air, licked his lips, and let out a loud whinny.

"He's a beauty," Andy declared, walking up to join them, and as he patted Winston on the neck, the big gelding dropped his head and rubbed it against Andy's chest.

"You really are a horse-whisperer," Carly exclaimed. "Look at that. He's taken to you already."

"You are one super-sized fella. Damn, Carly, I can't believe you ride him in a halter?"

"You should see her in person," Paul interjected. "She's incredible."

"That's somethin' I'm lookin' forward to, and if anyone's a horse-whisperer around here, seems like that would be you, Carly," Andy declared. "He's a lotta horse."

"Not really. He's as soft as cotton to ride. Come on, handsome," she said, beaming up at her best friend. "I have to take your shipping boots off and let you settle in. Thanks, Paul. I'll call you later. Have a safe trip back."

As she led Winston into the barn, she heard Paul start up a conversation with Andy, but she didn't stop to listen. She already knew what the outcome would be.

* * *

From the window of his office Keith had seen the big grey gelding step off the trailer. He was a gorgeous horse, but it wasn't Winston he was there to watch. It was Carly.

Her painted on jeans and long-sleeved T-shirt clung deliciously to her curves, and the frequent blush that crossed her face was adorable. Her blue eyes literally twinkled when she studied him, and that's what it seemed she did. Study him. Then there were her questions.

Her curiosity was to be expected, Sandy had been curious too, and Jenna before her, but Carly was different. Carly wasn't just curious. Carly was intrigued.

"Keith, do you want some coffee?"

Turning around, he saw Elsie standing at the door. He hadn't heard her come in. That wasn't normal.

"Yeah, thanks, coffee would be good."

"Are you watching her?"

"Not anymore. She's gone into the barn. Nice horse she's got. Real nice."

"Are you sure you did the right thing hiring that girl?"

"Nope, but she was the best candidate, and why are you askin' me that?"

"I've known you since the day you were born. You've taken a shine to her, that's why. I knew that when she first came here. That's not good, Keith."

"Everything will be fine, Elsie. She's not the type to go yappin' to the first person who asks her a question. That's the key. Findin' a woman with the right skill set who knows how to keep her mouth shut."

"I think you're probably right about that, but you're going to have to be careful. She's no dummy. Sandy wasn't either, but Sandy didn't care, especially after she met Mark."

"Yeah, I know all that. Don't worry. I know how to handle Carly Kincaid."

"Are you sure about that?" Elsie asked skeptically, frowning as she walked across to the desk. "Keith, you're so close to getting everything you want, everything you've worked for, now isn't the time to take chances."

"You're overreactin', and hirin' Carly isn't takin' a chance. I wouldn't have done it if I thought that. Relax. I'll keep her in check."

"Make sure you do. Do you want cinnamon coffee or regular?"

"Cinnamon, thanks, Elsie."

As she turned and left the office, Keith moved back to the window. The trailer had left, and Andy was walking down to the paddocks.

"This is good," he muttered. "Carly's exactly right for this place. In another week she'll be settled in and she'll be too busy to be intrigued. Still, it might be wise to nip things in the bud. Yeah, before dinner. She can sit uncomfortably for a short time. That should do it."

CHAPTER THREE

In spite of Elsie's reassuring words about dressing casually, Carly spent over an hour deciding what to wear to her welcome dinner. Finally choosing a long navy print dress with white pearl buttons down the front, white boots and a pale blue denim jacket, she took extra time with her curling iron and applying her makeup. Studying her reflection in the old-fashioned oval mirror, she was pleased with what she saw. Stepping outside, a blustery wind flirted with her long skirt, sending her hurrying around her truck and climbing behind the wheel.

Though excited about the evening she was a tad nervous, especially after receiving a text from Keith asking her to arrive fifteen minutes early. Driving up to the house, she checked the time with the old, battered Timex she'd owned since high school. It was almost six-forty-five. Stopping next to a gleaming black truck in the parking area, she grabbed the white purse she reserved for special occasions, walked hastily through the chilly wind to the front door.

"Welcome," Elsie said, opening it before Carly rang the bell. "In future you can just come on in. Keith is waiting for you in his office."

"Thank you, Elsie," Carly replied, stepping into the welcoming warmth. "Something smells delicious."

"With the weather suddenly turning chilly I decided to make chicken and dumplings, but there are plenty of veggies in there as well."

"That sounds wonderful."

"You'd best find out what Keith wants. I'll see you shortly."

Turning down the hall, she remembered how edgy she'd been the day of her interview. She'd wanted the job so much. Now it was hers and she couldn't be happier. Reaching his study, she knocked lightly, then stood waiting for his invitation to enter.

"I had to step out," he declared, startling her as he approached from behind.

Leaning past her and pushing the door open, he gestured for her to go in, but when he closed it behind them she saw him turn the lock. A shiver pricked her skin.

"I stopped in and checked on Winston," he said casually as he perched on the edge of his desk. "He's a gentle giant, and he looked very content."

"Change doesn't bother him. Probably because he spent his life at horse shows."

"I'm sure you're wonderin' why I asked you to come early."

"I am. I assume it must be important."

"It is. Take a seat."

He pointed at the chair directly in front of him. She momentarily paused. It would place her ridiculously close to him. Trying to ignore her butterflies she did as he asked, only to find his clasped hands resting in front of his crotch just a couple of feet away.

Lifting her gaze, she stared into his caramel eyes. A stern frown had crossed his brow. She suddenly felt as if she'd been summoned to the principal's office. She was about to be scolded, of that she was sure, but what had she done? The only thing she could think of was asking whether or not he owned the ranch.

She inwardly cringed.

It had been a stupid mistake.

"Do you remember the conversation we had when you first came here?"

"You mean at the interview?"

"Yep, at the interview."

"Which part of the conversation exactly?"

"Didn't I make it a point that you were to mind your own business and no-one else's?"

"Um, yes."

"Then why did you ask me a bunch of questions earlier?"

"I did?"

"You even had the nerve to ask if I owned this ranch."

"Was that bad?"

"Excuse me?" he said, raising his eyebrows. "Did you just ask if that was bad?"

"Sorry," she murmured, dropping her head as an annoying red blush crept across her cheeks.

"It doesn't matter if I own it, if I lease it, or if I work for someone else. All you need to know is that I'm your boss."

The faint scent of his cologne tickled her nostrils, and her gaze had settled on his hands. She hadn't noticed it before, but his nails were manicured. Whoever heard of a cowboy with manicured nails? What the hell was that about?

"I understand and I apologize," she said hastily, hoping she sounded appropriately contrite. "I didn't mean anything by it."

"That's hardly the point. I like you, Carly, but you won't last five minutes if you don't respect my privacy and the privacy of those who work here. If someone wants to volunteer something that's fine, but you're not to pry."

"Isn't this all a bit much?" she suddenly blurted out, lifting her eyes. "What's the big deal? Did you all rob a bank or something?"

She instantly regretted the outburst.

Her thoughts had tumbled through her head, and before she could stop them, the words had spilled from her lips. Wishing the floor would open and swallow her up, she tried to make it right.

"I'm so sorry," she said earnestly. "I've never been in a situation like this. Asking questions is just a part of being friendly and getting to know each other."

"I think you'd better leave," he declared, abruptly standing up and moving towards the windows behind his desk.

"Leave?" she repeated, a shard of panic making her heart thump. "Do you mean your office or—"

"I'm sorry, Carly, this is my fault," he said brusquely, keeping his back to her as he stared out at the night. "I misjudged you. You're not a fit for this ranch after all."

"Are you...are you firing me?" she muttered, barely able to speak.

"I am, and at this point I must remind you about the confidentiality agreement you signed."

She was just about to beg his forgiveness, when she was seized by an unexpected flash of anger.

"Dammit, this isn't fair!"

Watching him slowly turn around, a searing heat burned the back of her throat.

"Fair?" he repeated, moving towards her. "You knew my expectations. You said you understood and agreed to the terms and conditions I laid out, yet in the blink of an eye you chose to ignore them. Do you think that's fair? Or am I wrong? Did I make my wishes clear or didn't I?"

"You, uh, you did, and I'm truly sorry. Honestly. Please will you give me another chance? I won't ask anyone about anything unless it's related to the job, I swear."

He didn't respond, but stared at her.

A flicker of hope made her heart skip.

"Like I said, I've never been in a situation like this," she continued, desperately pleading her case. "Being curious is only human, but asking whether or not this ranch is yours, that was completely out of line. I was embarrassed then and I'm embarrassed now. I really want to stay, and if I mess up again I'll—"

"Do you remember the punishment for breaking the rules?"

"Uh...yes," she squeaked, her hot throat constricting and her stomach flipping.

"Tell me."

"Uh, c-corporal d-discipline," she stammered, her red face now blazing crimson.

"If you want to stay you'll have to accept the consequences. You broke the rules, and broke them badly."

"I understand."

"Are you saying you're willing to accept the punishment?"

"Uh, yes," she replied, though in a breathy voice she didn't recognize.

"Stand up and place your hands on the desk."

She wanted to do as he asked, but she felt weak, and she was sure her legs would be wobbly.

"Give me your hand."

As she accepted his offer, and his fingers wrapped around hers, she wanted to close her eyes and relish the moment.

His grip was strong, but not harsh, and his skin against hers was surprisingly soft. She could easily imagine his touch on her body, and as he pulled her to her feet something extraordinary happened. Though she was a tad fearful and certainly embarrassed, she had never been so turned on in her life.

"There," he declared, putting her hand firmly on the desk. "Now lay the other one next to it and scoot your feet out."

As she did as he directed, her breathing turned ragged, and staring down at the carpet, she was grateful her hair was falling around her face, hiding her scarlet cheeks.

"You can change your mind at any time," he said, wrapping his arm around her waist. "Just say stop and I will, but that will also be your resignation. Do you understand?"

"Yes, I understand."

"Then I'll begin."

His hand landed with a solid swat on her right cheek, then followed with another to the left. It was far more embarrassing than painful, and having her body in his firm grasp was making her pulse race as much as the humiliating spanking. He was delivering his slaps in a slow rhythm, and though the sting was increasing, she felt herself surrendering to the deliciously decadent feelings washing through her.

She wanted him to raise her skirt, lower her panties and spank her naked ass.

She wanted him to see the glistening wetness peeping through the backs of her thighs.

She wanted his fingers to explore her sex as he slapped.

Most of all—she wanted to feel his cock slide inside her soaked channel.

"Break the rules so badly again, and if I don't fire you I'll take a strap to your backside. Is that clear?"

"Very clear," she managed breathlessly, though every nerve in her body sparked, her heart thumped, her legs threatened to give way, and she ached for him to take her into his arms and hold her.

"Let this put an end to the matter," he said formally, but as he released her, to her great surprise and joy, he granted her unspoken, fervent wish. Helping her straighten up, he enveloped her in a warm, tender hug.

"I won't do anything like it again," she mumbled, devouring the feel of his hard body and muscled arms around her, arms she never wanted to leave.

"Catch your breath, then go down and join the others," he said softly, pulling back and looking down at her. "They'll probably be here by now and waitin' in the livin' room."

Gazing into his soft brown eyes, everything in her screamed to circle her hands around his neck, press her mouth on his, and devour him in an endless, ardent kiss.

"You want some water?" he asked, breaking into her salacious thoughts. "How about a spot of brandy to settle your nerves?"

"Brandy, thank you," she murmured, trying to catch her breath as he stepped away. "I am feeling a bit weird."

"That's only natural," he replied reassuringly, ambling to a tray on a sideboard holding two decanters and several glasses. "Have you ever been spanked before?"

"I thought we didn't ask questions?"

"Wrong. *You* don't ask, but *I* get to ask as many as I want," he declared, walking back and handing her the drink.

"That doesn't seem quite fair."

"Who said anything about the rules bein' fair? They are what they are. So, have you?"

"Not like that," she muttered, then gratefully taking a swallow of the comforting liquor, she closed her eyes and let the soothing warmth slide down her throat. "Thank you. I haven't eaten much today so I'd better not drink much more."

"You feelin' okay to join the others?"

"Sure," she replied, placing her glass on the desk, though she wasn't sure at all.

"If you need the powder room, it's third on the left down the hall."

"So, I, uh, I guess I'll see you at dinner."

"Yep. See you at dinner."

Picking up her bag, she turned to leave, but to her surprise he walked with her and opened the door.

"Don't worry, Carly, no-one will have any idea what just happened," he said softly, "not unless you tell them, and that's confidential, so you won't, right?"

"Right. Besides, I have no absolutely no desire for anyone to find out," she replied, then feeling brave enough to look at him, she added, "Thank you for the second chance. I won't let you down."

"You're welcome. I don't believe you will, but you know what will happen if you do."

Nodding, then starting down the hall, she could feel his eyes on her, but when she stopped at the powder room and looked back, he was gone.

Moving inside the small room, she stared at her reflection. Her face was still flushed. Turning on the faucet, she ran her wrists under the cold running water. It was a trick she'd learned to cool down on a hot day. It worked, but as she dried off and headed to the living room, she sensed she'd crossed an invisible line. A line from which there was no turning back.

CHAPTER FOUR

Elsie's food was delicious, the conversation at the dinner table free-flowing and easy, and Carly felt a sparkling connection to the handsome cowboy sitting across from her.

Whenever Keith caught her eye a thrill pulsed through her body. The spanking had been intensely erotic, and she couldn't deny her deep attraction. In an attempt to take her mind off the wetness between her legs, and her desperate desire to be wrapped up in his arms, she turned her attention to Andy and Salvo.

She suspected Andy was at least a decade older than Keith. He was the most serious of the three men. But after a glass of wine a sardonic sense of humor emerged, and several times he had everyone in stitches. His weathered face bore witness of long hours in the saddle, and he carried himself with the confidence of a man comfortable in his own skin. His eyes were hazel, the surrounding skin deeply wrinkled. She guessed he didn't like sunglasses. He wasn't tall or as powerfully built as Keith and Salvo, but she had the feeling he was just as strong.

Wearing a crisp white shirt, Salvo was surprisingly attractive, with thick, curly black hair and bright blue eyes. He was more urban than country, and she wondered how he'd ended up on a ranch. Though he was the low man on the totem pole, Andy and Keith didn't talk down to him, and when he spoke, they listened attentively. He was the first to thank Elsie for the meal and excuse himself, but Carly wasn't surprised. He was responsible for feeding early in the morning.

"Here's your container," Elsie declared, leaving the table and fetching a plastic bowl from the sideboard. "That should help keep you fed until Sunday."

"Thanks so much, Elsie."

"Always my pleasure."

"Every Sunday Elsie delivers a feast," Andy explained as Salvo left the room. "We keep notes as the days go by, then get together and go over things. You need to do that as well."

"What a good idea," Carly said. "That will also help me keep track of the horses as well. It's so easy to forget things, and there's a lot to remember around here."

"That there is," Andy muttered with a nod, then stifled a yawn. "I'm gonna turn in. The four horses you'll be ridin' tomorrow are on the board, and you can climb on Winston whenever it suits you."

"Only four?"

"Yep. We have clients comin' to check out three over the weekend, and I need to put them through their paces. The other three I'm still trainin'. I don't want anyone else on their backs till I'm done. Your first couple of weeks here will be light."

"Okay. I'll see you tomorrow then."

"Yep, and I'm real happy to have you here."

"Thanks, Andy."

"Night Keith, night Elsie, thanks for another delicious supper."

"My pleasure, Andy," Elsie replied, walking across to peck him on the cheek.

As Carly watched him walk into the hall and head to his bedroom, she thought it curious that he lived in the house. It crossed her mind he and Keith might be partners, but immediately reminded herself it was none of her business.

"Can I help you clean up?" Carly asked as Elsie began clearing the table.

"Thank you, my dear, but no," Elsie said adamantly. "I don't like people in my kitchen."

"I wouldn't argue if I were you," Keith remarked with a grin. "Come on, I'll walk you out to your truck."

"Thank you, Elsie," Carly said gratefully, giving her a hug. "That was a wonderful dinner, the best I've had in a long time."

"I'm glad you enjoyed it. I'll be seeing you at noon Sunday. Don't be late."

"I wouldn't dream of it."

She'd taken off her denim jacket, and as she picked it up from the back of her chair, Keith took it from her hands and held it open for her.

"This won't keep you warm," he said solemnly. "The forecast called for a cold, windy night."

"I don't have far to go. I'll be fine."

"We don't want you gettin' sick."

"I won't," she said, smiling up at him as she turned around. "I appreciate your concern though."

"What time will you be gettin' on your horse?" he asked as they started into the foyer. "I'd like to watch."

"Probably around eleven o'clock. That's been our routine."

"Then you should keep it that way. Horses like routine."

"I agree. Yikes, listen to that weather," she muttered as they approached the front door. "I didn't hear it over dinner."

"Our fall winds must be startin'. Better prepare yourself. They can get mighty strong."

She buttoned up her jacket, but when they stepped outside, even though she was ready for it, a startlingly strong gust sent her face into his chest.

"Good grief. It's like a tornado."

"Almost," he said, quickly placing his arm around her shoulders. "Keep your head down and stick close to me."

With the powerful winds swirling around them, she huddled against him as they walked hastily to the motor court, but had to step back as he struggled to open her door and hold it steady. Hurriedly climbing behind the wheel, she let out a relieved breath.

"That's unbelievable!" she exclaimed as he gripped the door and leaned his head inside the cab. "I've never been in wind like that."

"Drive slowly back to the cabin," he shouted, his head inside the cab. "Hopefully this will pass overnight."

His face was inches from hers.

Impulsively she pecked him on the cheek.

He didn't back away, but turned to catch her eyes.

Her heart skipped.

He was going to kiss her.

She was sure of it—but he blinked.

The moment passed...

"Drive safe," he muttered, then backed out, closed her door.

Trying to calm her racing heart, she started up the truck and rolled cautiously forward, but continued to watch him fight his way back to the house. As he disappeared inside and she started down the driveway, the magic moment replayed itself in her head.

His voice had been husky.

Sexy husky.

"I hope it was because you felt what I did," she muttered. "It wasn't just my imagination. I know it!"

She'd reached the short lane that led to the carport, but as she turned, a fierce gust wobbled her truck, startling her and making her slam on the brakes. Fruitless against the turbulent winds, her precious pickup began to rock violently. Frozen in fear, her fingers gripped the wheel in a white-knuckle grip.

A flash caught her eye.

Glancing up, the headlights showed a branch flying through the air...heading straight towards her.

* * *

Salvo was finishing his nightly pushups when he thought he heard a crash. Leaping to his feet and grabbing his phone, he called Keith as he raced outside.

"Salvo? What's up?"

"I heard something. It sounded like a car wreck. I'm outside but it's so dark and there's so much wind...shit. There are lights above Carly's cabin. I think they're headlights. I'm going over there."

"I'm on my way."

Calling Andy and telling him to meet him at his truck, Keith bolted from his bedroom, pausing only to grab his heavy winter jacket from the closet in the foyer. Stepping outside, he was shocked at the ferocity of the winds. Struggling through them to his truck, he barely managed to open the door and climb inside. Leaving the parking area, he stopped under the portico just as Andy ran out the front door.

"What the hell's goin' on?" Andy asked breathlessly as he climbed into the passenger seat.

"Salvo called. He heard some kind of crash, and when he went outside he saw the headlights of Carly's pickup."

"Dammit. I'll bet she's been hit by flyin' debris," Andy exclaimed. "It's a crazy night."

"We may as well be in a fuckin' tornado," Keith grunted as he expertly sped down the drive. "God I hope she's—oh, no!"

His truck's powerful lights lit up a terrifying scene. A branch had pierced Carly's windshield, and Salvo was frantically trying to open the driver's door.

"No, no, no!" Keith yelled, jumping from his truck and dashing through the wind.

"I think she's okay," Salvo exclaimed. "She's awake, but I can't get the door open."

"Fetch the crowbar from my truck, and hurry," Keith barked, then leaned over the hood and stared through the broken glass into the cab. "Carly! Carly can you hear me?"

He could see her nod, but she didn't speak.

"Is she hurt?" Andy shouted, reaching Keith's side.

"I don't know. We've gotta get in there, but the damn door's jammed. Try the passenger side."

"Hey, Keith, you're panickin'. Take a breath."

Darting his head around and seeing Andy's steely control. Keith had never been so grateful for his best friend's presence.

"We'll get her out, but you've gotta stay calm."

"You're right. Of course you're right," Keith said hastily. "Sorry."

"Watch where you put your hands," Andy shouted sharply. "There's glass everywhere. Are there any gloves in your truck?"

"Yeah, in the center console, and a pair in the tool box in the cab."

"Stay calm. You need to for her. I'll be right back."

"Sorry, Keith," Salvo declared, running up to him as Andy left and giving him a flashlight. "I should have left this with you."

"Thanks. Be careful where you put your hands, and keep your eyes open. There's crap flying everywhere. I see you got the crowbar? Try the passenger door. You might have better luck."

As Keith shone the light into the small dark space, Carly twisted her head around and stared at him.

His heart leapt.

Her face was white, and her eyes were filled with fear and anguish, but she was alive. Giving her the thumbs up, he shone the powerful beam over her body. The branch had smashed through the window and hit her arm, pinning her down. It had missed her torso by inches.

"This is a miracle," he muttered.

"The door's moving," Salvo suddenly yelled.

Bolting around the truck to help, Keith placed the flashlight on the ground, and gripped the crow bar next to Salvo.

"On three," Keith shouted. "One, two, three."

It made a dreadful creaking sound as it opened, then jammed and wouldn't go any further, but there was enough space for Keith to lean inside.

"Carly, I'm here," he said, wondering how they'd move her without cutting her to pieces.

"K-Keith, I'm s-scared," she stammered breathlessly. "C-can you g-get me out?"

"You bet, but try to stay calm. Are you in any pain?"

"M-my arm, but not too b-bad. I've been afraid to m-move. I d-didn't know what would happen if I d-did."

"That was smart. Good girl."

"Thank G-God you came," she sputtered, tears spilling down her face. "I thought I was g-going to be t-trapped all night."

"Easy does it. We're all here and we're gonna have you out real quick. Just hang on. I hear Andy callin'. I'll be right back."

"I promise n-not to go anywhere."

Her brave quip melted his heart.

Cautiously stepping back, he saw Andy striding towards him holding another flashlight.

"Hey, Andy."

"How is she?" Andy asked, handing Keith a pair of gloves. "What's the story?"

"I think she's okay, and the branch doesn't seem wedged. It looks like it's just restin' on top of the dashboard and pressin' against her arm. If we can get the driver's door open, and find somethin' for me to lie on to give me support and some height, I can push up the branch like I'm doin' a bench press and you can help her out the passenger door. We only need a few inches."

"Let me do that," Salvo exclaimed, stepping up to join them. "I'll hold it up while you get her out."

"No, no way," Keith said firmly, shaking his head. "If something goes wrong—"

"Keith, he's younger and stronger than you are, and he lifts weights," Andy interjected. "Salvo, there's an ottoman by the fireplace in the cabin that should put you at the right height. While you're in there, see if there's a hand sweep to brush the glass off the seat."

"Andy! What the hell?" Keith protested as Salvo hurried down to the cabin.

"Hey, we can't lose you."

"We can't lose him either."

"Less likely," Andy said solemnly. "We both know he can bench press more than you."

"True," Keith reluctantly agreed, "but all this is pointless if we can't get that driver's door open. Why don't you give it a try? I wanna talk to her and let her know what's happenin'."

"You read my mind," Andy said, reaching for the crowbar, but as he did, a howling gust blasted around them. "Damn winds. Seems like they're gettin' worse."

"I think you're right. We need to make this happen fast."

As Andy started around the pickup, Keith leaned into the cab, reminding himself to keep his voice calm.

"Hey, Carly, we've figured out how to do this. Don't worry, this will be a piece of cake. How are you doin'? Any trouble breathin'? Can you move your fingers and toes? Any tinglin'?"

"I'm okay. I'm just s-scared my arm m-might be b-broken."

"Take it easy," he said softly. "This is what we're gonna do. There's glass on the seat. We're gonna get that outta the way, then we're gonna lift the log and slide you out from under. Like I said, a piece of cake. It won't take long."

"That sounds g-good. S-sorry," she said, stifling a sob, "I was okay, but now I'm not."

"You're doin' great. Just hold on a few more minutes."

Pulling back, he found Salvo waiting with a small sweep brush and the ottoman on the ground beside him. Wordlessly handing Keith the brush, Salvo picked up the ottoman and hurried across to the drivers side.

"Carly, it won't be long now," Keith said confidently, popping his head back in. "I'm gonna brush this glass outta the way."

"Keith, if anything bad happens..."

"Hey, we're almost there. I'll be slidin' you across this seat in just a few minutes."

"But th-things can g-go wrong. What if the branch f-falls on me?"

"It won't."

"But it might, and, uh, Keith, I n-need you to know—I th-think you're amazing, I, uh, I like you. I like you a lot."

"Carly..."

But the sound of protesting metal startled them both. Salvo and Andy had wrenched open the driver's door.

CHAPTER FIVE

Minutes later Keith helped Carly maneuver away from the heavy branch. When Salvo lowered it back down, it didn't crash, but rested on top of the dashboard. Carly may have been trapped, but she hadn't borne the weight of the onerous log. Though bruised and in pain, she didn't appear to be badly injured, but Keith immediately swept her up and carried her to his truck.

"Just take me to my cabin," she stammered. "All I need is to go to bed."

"Don't talk nonsense," he said firmly as he pushed his way through the blustery winds.

"Really, I'm fine."

"Elsie's a nurse, and she's gonna check you out, and you're spendin' the night in the house where we can keep an eye on you."

"But I'm fine, honest," she repeated. "I don't want to be—"

"We don't know that. At the very least you're probably in shock."

Andy had been speaking to Salvo, but caught up just in time to open the passenger door.

"Keith's right," he declared as Keith set her gently down on the seat. "You need to be given the once-over."

"I'm just a bit shaken up, that's all."

"Carly, you don't need to prove you're tough," he said reassuringly, climbing in next to her. "There are times you need to let others take care of you. This is one of those times."

Keith was fighting to open his door, and finally succeeding, he slammed it shut and sucked in a long breath.

"This is about as bad as it gets," he muttered with a deep frown. "Have you ever seen it like this, Andy?"

"A couple of years back. Don't you remember? That tree came down."

"Oh, yeah. That was one helluva windstorm. Looks like this one's fixin' to match it. You'd better call Elsie and let her know we're on our way back."

"Yep, I was about to do that very thing. Let's get outta here before another branch comes flyin' our way."

As Keith began driving through the dark, dangerous night, Carly laid her head back and closed her eyes. Every part of her trembled, she felt sick to her stomach, her head was pounding, and a heavy ache rippled through her shoulder and arm.

But somehow she'd survived.

The first few minutes of her horrifying ordeal had been surreal, and when she'd found herself held down by the branch, she'd been seized with the terror of not being found until morning—if she even survived that long.

Though she'd fought the growing panic, she'd been losing the battle when a miraculous beam of light had filled the cab. Seeing Salvo's face peering through the window, she'd broken into heavy sobs, but by the time Keith arrived she'd managed to pull herself together. She'd tried to maintain a brave front, but when he'd tried to comfort her, she'd been unable to stop the tears.

The short drive to the house seemed to take forever. She'd never been so cold or thirsty, and craved the comfort of a man's arms around her. But not just any man. She wanted Keith. She wanted to crawl into bed with him and stay snuggled against his chest until the sun rose in the morning.

"How are you feelin'?" Andy asked as the truck rolled to a stop beneath the portico.

"Fine. Just cold."

"You're as white as a ghost," he remarked, studying her face. "You're not fine at all."

With the wind swirling around him, Keith jumped from behind the wheel and hurried around the truck to hold the door for Andy, but as he climbed down, Carly quickly followed.

The moment her foot hit the step, her legs buckled.

Falling sideways against Keith, he released his fierce grip on the door to scoop her up, but darting behind him Andy caught it as it flew backwards, then fighting the gusts he managed to get it closed.

Carrying Carly swiftly to the front door, to Keith's great relief Elsie opened it and he strode inside. Hurrying down the hall and into the guest room, he laid Carly gently on the bed. Only then did he notice the bloody gash beneath her torn jacket.

"Go into the kitchen and warm up some milk," Elsie said briskly. "Splash in some brandy, and make sure you knock when you come back."

"Just one-second," he said, his voice turning soft. "I wanna tell this little lady we're gonna take real good care of her."

As he sat on the edge of the bed and took her hand, a lone tear slid from the side of her eye.

"Hey, you're safe. The drama is over."

"What I said when you, uh..."

"Hush now. You need to rest. Tomorrow's a new day and you'll feel a whole lot better."

"But, uh, please don't let what I said make things weird between us."

"I won't," he said warmly, then leaning in he whispered, "I feel the same."

The hint of a smile crossed her lips, and he spied a light in her red-rimmed eyes.

"She's all yours, Elsie," he murmured, releasing Carly's hand and rising to his feet. "Fix her up. We need her in the saddle."

"She'll be just fine," Elsie assured him, "but you need to go now."

"Yes, ma'am."

But he didn't want to go anywhere.

He wanted to stay and watch over her.

But turning around he reluctantly left the room and headed down the hall. Salvo had been the hero of the night, and Keith could not have been more proud. The lost, unruly teenager he'd taken off the streets had grown into a courageous, caring, responsible young man.

"Hey, there, you wanna join me?" Andy asked as Keith entered the kitchen.

Lifting his eyes, he found Andy at the table nursing a whisky with the bottle in front of him.

"Damn straight," Keith replied, retrieving a tumbler from the cabinet. "This has been a helluva night."

"I can't believe she wasn't killed," Andy said gravely as Keith sat opposite him. "Whatta the chances? She must have been a hair's breath from that log crushin' her."

"No shit!" Keith muttered. "She had an angel watchin' over her. Looks like she has a bad gash near her shoulder, but outside of that I think she's okay, though she's gotta be traumatized. I owe Salvo big time. If it hadn't been for him she'd still be out there."

"What did Elsie have to say?"

"She was optimistic, but that's how she is."

"Keith, in all the years I've known you, I've never seen you panic before."

"I've never seen a girl trapped in a car with a goddamned tree trunk through her windshield before," Keith retorted, then taking another drink he looked at his friend and narrowed his eyes. "Whatta you tryin' to say, Andy?"

"I'm not tryin' to say anything, I'm just wonderin' if you might be..."

"Might be what?"

"Takin' a shine to her."

Keith didn't answer, but ran his fingers through his thick mop of dark hair, then took another drink.

"I guess that answers that question," Andy quipped. "I'm glad. You've had your guard up too long."

"I haven't let my guard down," Keith said hastily. "You know I can't get involved. Truth is, I tried to fire her before dinner."

"Why?"

"Why do you think? What you just said," he admitted grimly, "and she was askin' too many questions."

"But you didn't, did you?"

"No, dammit! I didn't want her to go."

"Is this attraction mutual?"

"Yeah, she's already told me. She told me before we got her out from under that branch, but that was probably because she was scared."

"The truth has a habit of comin' out when we think we're about to meet our maker. What'd you tell her?"

"Dammit."

"Dammit? You told her dammit? You sure are usin' that word a lot."

"I told her I felt the same," Keith said with a heavy sigh. "What the hell do I do about this?"

"Whatta you wanna do?"

"What I want and what is...is...uh..."

"Safe?"

"Yeah, what is safe, they're two different things. I can't take that risk."

"Sure you can."

"What did you just say?"

"I said, sure you can," Andy said with the hint of a grin.

"Hey, if I'm exposed you are too, and you have as much to lose as I do."

"We've been playin' this cat and mouse game for too long. We've both found ways to scratch our itch, but Keith, I wanna come home to a woman besides Elsie, and I reckon you're feelin' that way too."

"I know, I know, but we're almost there. That's the problem. We're so close this isn't the time to take chances."

"Let me ask you somethin'. When was the last time you had a heart-stoppin' holy crap moment with a woman? Isn't that what's happened with Carly?"

Keith paused, splashed some more whisky into his glass, then slowly nodded his head.

"The minute she walked into my office a month ago," he murmured. "I knew right then I should've hired someone else, but I thought if I kept her at arm's length I could handle it."

"And how's that workin' for you?"

"Dammit, Andy."

"There's that word again."

"That word is how I'm feelin'!"

"Someone's gotta straighten out that pretzeled head of yours."

"What the hell am I supposed to do? I can't tell her what's goin' on."

"Because?"

"I'm not gonna put that burden on her."

"You might have a point. Okay, Keith, tell me, how close are we gettin' to the end of his charade? How soon do you think we'll be able to come clean without risk?"

"There'll always be risk, you know how powerful he is, but a few more big sales and we'll be debt free and this place will be paid for. A few more after that, and we'll have cash in the bank. That's what I want, cash in the bank. Then if he tries to pull any shit we'll have the funds to fight him."

"Has it ever occurred to you he won't?"

"Andy, I'm the heir apparent. When I bail, he'll have a complete meltdown."

"True, but if we're only half-a-dozen horses away, there's no reason you can't let things with Carly develop. You can keep our secret for a little while, and she's not likely to fly off to Houston and find out who you are."

"But don't I have to tell her?" Keith asked, staring at his friend. "She thinks I'm just a rancher. When she finds out who I am, I won't be that person anymore."

"First, I think your underestimatin' her. Second, a name and all the crap that goes with it doesn't change who you are. That's just bein' paranoid. Third, and most importantly, when was the last time you met someone who made your heart pump? I'd go for it, and on that note I'm off to bed," he declared, downing the last of his whisky.

"Hang on! What's the bottom line?"

"It's up to you, but I'd let this thing with Carly crinkle out. You'll know if and when the time is right to reveal everything."

"Yeah. That's good advice, Andy. Thanks."

"One last thing. If you do reach that point, prepare yourself. She'll be pissed you didn't fill her in sooner, but that's the way it has to be. It'll work out one way or another. Just don't jump the gun. See you in the mornin'."

Watching his friend amble from the room, Keith picked up his whisky, stared into the amber liquor, and let his mind wander.

Carly made his pulse race and his cock stiffen.

When he'd spanked her, he'd ached to lift her skirt, pull down her panties, gaze at her backside, then mercilessly ravage her.

As he'd pulled her into his arms, he'd wanted to consume her mouth and roam his hands over her luscious body.

All through dinner he'd had an erection.

Her joyous laugh and sparkle in her eye had utterly captivated him.

"Where's that milk and brandy?"

Startled, he darted his head up.

"Sorry, Elsie," he apologized, looking at her sheepishly as she walked across to the refrigerator. "Andy was here. I got sidetracked. How's Carly? Can I see her? Can I take the drink into her?"

"The milk and brandy is for me, not her," Elsie replied with a smile. "I gave her a sedative. She's sleeping. Her arm will be sore for a few days. There's bruising and a large abrasion near her shoulder, but it's superficial. Otherwise she's fine. I swear, she has to be the luckiest woman alive."

"Alive being the key word," Keith muttered. "Talk about a miracle. Damn, I'm beat."

"Me too," Elsie mumbled with a sigh, placing the glass of milk she'd poured into the microwave. "Keith, even though I still believe there's risk, I think I've changed my mind."

"Excuse me?" he said, jerking up his head.

"I'm saying you could do a lot worse than Carly Kincaid, and let's face it, this race you've been running...you've turned the corner and you're heading for home."

CHAPTER SIX

Stretched out on his bed listening to the windstorm wail its wrath, Keith found himself consumed with thoughts of the spunky, brave, beautiful girl down the hall. He barely knew her. Why couldn't he get her out of his mind? Why did he yearn for her naked body next to his?

"This is crazy," he grunted, slipping from his bed and pulling on his robe. "What the hell is wrong with me?"

Milk and brandy was Elsie's sure-fire sleeping tonic. Deciding he'd follow her example he left his room and padded down the hall, but as he passed Carly's room he thought he heard her calling his name.

Pausing, he put his ear to the door.

He heard her again.

Gently knocking, he cautiously poked his head in. She was tossing and turning, obviously in the throes of a bad dream. Hurrying across the room he sat on the edge of the bed and placed his hands on her shoulders.

"Hey, Carly, wake up! You're okay. You're dreamin.'"

"No, please, I don't want to die here...no...Keith! Keith!"

Hating to see her in such distress, he pulled her into his arms he held her tightly against his body.

"Wake up, Carly, I'm here, you're okay, I'm here."

"Keith?"

Abruptly pulling back, she stared up at him, then her eyes darted around the room.

"You're in my house," he said gently. "You were havin' a nightmare."

"But...I was in Daisy, I was trapped," she muttered, "I couldn't get out. I was so scared."

"I know, but you're safe now."

"I'm safe," she mumbled, falling back against him. "I'm so glad you're here."

"That's what you said when I found you."

"I've never been so happy to see anyone in my life."

"Except maybe Salvo holdin' the flashlight."

"Yeah," she muttered, "him too. Thank God for you both."

"You feelin' better?"

"Uh-huh, but my heart is still thumping," she murmured, raising her head and gazing up at him. "How did you know to come in here?"

"I was on my way to the kitchen when I heard you cryin' out."

Bathed in the soft glow from the night-lights, her eyes carried a silver sparkle.

His heart swelled.

"Do you think you can get some sleep now?" he asked, wishing he could crawl into bed with her.

"Um, yes, but can I ask a favor? I still feel shaky. Would you mind lying next to me and holding me for just a few minutes?"

She had tentatively whispered her request, and though his brain rattled a thousand reasons why he should walk away, he heard himself say,

"I think I can manage that."

As she slipped from his arms to lie back down, he couldn't take his eyes off her. Even in the dim light he could see her nipples pressing urgently against the thin fabric of the nightgown Elsie must have given her. Fighting the aching need to lift it over her head and lower his mouth to her luscious breasts, he climbed under the covers, but with his robe tied around his body.

She curled against his chest.

His cock stirred.

He needed to leave.

But he wrapped his arms around her.

Even with his robe on, even though he hadn't touched her, even though he'd been able to fight a deep, yearning need to press his lips against hers in a fervent kiss, he knew it was too late.

They had crossed a line and there was no going back.

~ ~ ~ ~ ~ ~ ~ ~ ~

In Houston Texas it was 7 a.m.

Harlan Boyd, CEO of Boyd Holdings, was padding into his bathroom. Though he'd been on an international call until 1 a.m., he had a conference call at 8 a.m., and needed to be in his office with his lawyers fifteen minutes ahead of time.

His lack of sleep was legendary.

Many of his office staff believed he secretly napped during the day, but Harlan Boyd thrived on work. What others saw as stressful negotiations, Harlan saw as fun. Challenge energized him, solving problems made him feel alive, and debating people was fuel for his constantly churning brain.

There was, however, one challenge that was the source of constant frustration.

His son.

His brilliant, impossible, infuriating, renegade son.

As the waterfall shower streamed over him, he returned to the debate he'd been having with himself for several years. If he gave his rebellious boy enough space, he'd come to his senses and stop his wandering ways. At some point he'd return to the luxurious suite of offices from which Boyd Holdings operated.

But Harlan was running out of patience.

"Dammit, you need to start settling down," he muttered as he turned off the faucets. "I've had enough. After we finish our business this morning we're going to have a serious talk."

Toweling off, he walked into his closet, dressed in a charcoal grey pin-striped suit, crisp white shirt and red tie, and selected a watch from many on display in a burled walnut box.

"Harlan, honey?"

Turning around he saw his live-in girlfriend leaning against the door frame. She was curvy, beautiful, and half his age. He suspected his money and mansion contributed to her presence, but she was a thoughtful girl, and he enjoyed the comfort of her warm body and pleasant company.

"Yeah, Mitzi?"

"Do you have to leave so early?"

"You knew I was a busy man when you moved in," he said briskly. "You can't start complaining about it now."

"You're in one of your moods!"

"Nope. I just have things on my mind."

"Things? Don't you mean your son? You only bark at me when he's on your mind."

"He's done enough wandering, dammit. He needs to come home, and stay home! I'll be retiring in a couple of years. He has to be ready to take over and he still has a lot to learn."

"Maybe he doesn't want to take over. Maybe that's what he's been trying to tell you with his constant traveling."

"Or maybe his old man has been too soft," Harlan retorted. "I don't even know where he goes when he disappears, but I've had enough and I'm going to find out. For all I know he could have a wife and kids stashed away someplace. He sure hasn't shown any serious interest in the women around here. Anyway, I can't stand here talking. I need to get to the office."

"Harlan, honey?"

"What?"

"Do you want me to have a word with him?"

"You?"

"I know I'm not much older than him, but we've become friends. Maybe he'd open up to me. Maybe he'd tell me why he stays away like he does."

"I'll give it some thought, but now I have to dash. Go shopping, enjoy yourself, and don't forget we have dinner at Tony's tonight."

"I won't forget. I love that place."

"You should. It costs enough."

Marching through the bedroom, he trotted down the stairs and stepped out into the sweeping driveway fronting his magnificent home. His limousine waited, and his driver hurried to open the back door. Sliding into the back seat, Harlan thought about his son's mother.

Mabel. The love of his life.

They'd been college sweethearts, and their marriage had been a happy, loving union, but too early she'd fallen victim to cancer. All his money and power could do nothing to save her. It had been the only time in his life he'd felt helpless.

"I know what you'd say," he mumbled. "You'd tell me to let him be and forge his own path, but I built Boyd Holdings for him. Petroleum is in his blood, just like business is in his blood. He just has to stick around the office long enough to get into the swing of things, then he'd know it like I know it. Sorry, sweetheart, I'm going to put my foot down. He's coming home next week, and this time he's staying."

* * *

Keith had fallen into a deep sleep.

He hadn't meant to.

He had meant to slip quietly from the room when he knew Carly was at peace, but the fatigue from the night's traumatic events had taken their toll. When he opened his eyes and realized the sun was up, he glanced urgently at the clock on the bedside table. 8:23 a.m.

"Oh, no, the call," he muttered, panic seizing him. "I missed the damn call."

Softly moaning, Carly clung to his arm as he tried to move away.

"No, please don't leave, please, not yet."

"Sorry, I didn't mean to wake you," he said softly. "How do you feel?"

"Like I want to stay here with you forever," she murmured, curling against him.

"Elsie will be comin' to check on you soon—if she hasn't already. Damn, I can't believe I slept through the night."

"Does it matter?"

"Yeah, I missed an important call at six."

"I mean, does it matter about Elsie?"

"Uh...sort of, not really. Actually, I don't know the answer to that."

"She works for you, right? So why would she care?"

"Things aren't that simple, and I need to get up. How's your arm?"

"It hurts a bit, but Keith..."

"Yeah?"

"Thank you for staying with me. Is it okay for me to say I loved sleeping with you?"

Her voice was breathy, and as she raised her lips to languidly kiss his neck, his semi-stiff cock surged to attention.

"I really need to go, and you need to get more rest," he said firmly, trying to extricate himself from her limbs.

"Can't you stay just five more minutes?"

"Carly," he said, lowering his voice, "we both know if I stay five more minutes, Elsie will walk in on something she shouldn't."

"Not if you lock the door."

"Who are you? Who kidnapped the girl I hired?"

"We all have more than one side to us," she whispered, slipping her fingers under his disheveled robe.

"You know you're being a brat, right?"

"Are you complaining?"

"You, young lady, went through a terrible ordeal last night," he said sternly, ignoring her question. "I'm not sure you're as well as you think you are."

"I'm well enough to know you don't want to leave."

"I cannot believe—"

"That I'm being so pushy? Sometimes I have a problem keeping my feelings to myself."

"Obviously."

"But that doesn't mean they're not sincere."

"Keep this up and you'll be in for a hot backside the minute you're better."

"Promise?" she quipped, twinkling up at him.

"You are unbelievable," he grunted, finally managing to extricate himself and crawl from the bed. "I'm leavin', and you stay right where you are."

"Uh-huh."

"I'll see you soon."

"Wait."

"Now what?" he asked, straightening out his robe.

"You can't leave without kissing me goodbye."

"Sure I can."

"If you don't I'll tell everyone you stayed here."

"Blackmail?"

"A girl has to do what a girl has to do."

Sitting on the edge of the bed, he lifted her arm and studied the bandage.

"Carly, how can you possibly be feelin' this good after what you went through last night?"

"I'm a bouncer."

"Excuse me?"

"My mother always said I was a bouncer. Some kids fall over and skin their knee and cry for an hour. I'd jump back up and keep playing. When I was learning how to ride, if I fell off I didn't care. I'd bounce right up and climb back on. I'm a bouncer."

"I should have known. What about your arm?"

"Yeah, it hurts, but so what? When did a sore arm ever get in the way of a kiss?"

"I can't believe what I'm hearin'."

"You know kissing me is inevitable," she said softly, locking his eyes as she leaned into him. "You're feeling what I am. I know you are."

"You sure know a lot, young lady."

"Tell me I'm wrong."

"The only thing I'm tellin' you is that I've gotta leave," he said firmly, rising to his feet. "I'll check back on you later."

"Or maybe I'll check on you."

"Keep talkin' that way and I'll stay, but to spank your butt, and you may not want me to," he said sternly. "Get some rest, and that's an order."

Cracking open the door, he peered down the hallway.

There was no-one in sight.

With his cock screaming for attention, he hurried back to his bedroom, walked swiftly into his bathroom, dropped his robe and stepped into the shower. Carly's unabashed attitude was surprising, but he had to admit it was a total turn-on.

He wanted her.

He wanted to ravage her.

He wanted to devour her breasts and consume her pussy.

Closing his eyes, he wrapped his fingers around his cock and began to stroke.

"Can I help you with that?"

His eyes popped open.

She was naked and stepping into the stall.

"I know I shouldn't be here," she purred, moving close to him and wrapping her arms around his neck, "but sometimes..."

CHAPTER SEVEN

Keith's first impulse was to wallop Carly's ass and march her back to her bedroom, but his lips were suddenly on hers, and his hands were traveling feverishly over her naked body. Abruptly breaking their kiss, he moved his lips to suck her neck like a hungry vampire.

"God, I want you so much," she bleated, ignoring the hot water soaking her bandage and stinging her arm. "I want you to devour me."

Her comment sent the blood pumping through his loins.

Placing his arm around her waist and holding her tightly, he settled on the bench seat and ordered her to straddle his thighs.

"That doesn't mean sit on my cock," he growled as she moved her leg across him. "Just rest on my thighs."

He heard a disappointed whimper, but as he clutched her breasts and sucked in a nipple, she let out a loud moan and arched her back.

"You need to be kept in check," he said huskily, lifting his head and locking her eyes. "You're gonna learn to listen."

"I'll try," she whispered. "Uh, please, Keith, may I stroke your cock?"

A wicked smile curled the edges of his lips.

She had asked permission.

"Sit here a second," he muttered, shifting her off his lap and on to the seat next to him.

Rising to his feet, he turned off the faucets, then opening the stall door and grabbing the nearest towel, he folded it into a pad and placed it on the marble floor.

"Kneel on that and take me in your mouth," he instructed, sitting back down.

Moving swiftly from the bench, she positioned herself in front of him, then lowered her lips around his rock-hard rod. Curling his fingers into her wet hair, he was about to guide her salacious sucking when he spotted her hand slip between her legs.

"You only touch yourself when I say," he said firmly, griping her wrist and pulling it away. "Your job is to pleasure my cock, not your pussy. Hold me with both hands and lick the head."

She immediately swirled her tongue around the top of his penis, then opened her mouth and drew him in. A sudden surge of energy sparked through his loins, and as she increased the pace of her bobbing head he knew he wouldn't be able to keep his climax at bay if she continued the luscious licking.

"Get on all fours," he said gruffly.

"You mean, on my hands and knees?" she asked breathlessly, lifting her eyes and staring up at him.

"Now, with your ass towards me."

It was obvious she'd never been with a dominant man, and the sparkle in her eyes told him he was making her toes curl and her heart race. As she hastily took up the position, he smoothed his palm over her wet cheeks, then delivered the first slap.

She yelped, but wriggled as if asking for more.

He landed the second.

In spite of the hard marble, she spread her knees off the soft towel and arched her back. The silent invitation sent his hand slapping with swift, sharp smacks, then he paused to gaze at her swollen pussy and glistening wetness.

"Play with your clit, and make yourself come," he rasped, squeezing and fondling her reddened backside, then slid his fingers into her hot, open channel.

"Keith, ooh, Keith...I'm already so close."

"Stop!" he ordered gruffly, landing several hard swats with his free hand.

Continuing to vigorously finger her, he took hold of his cock and shifted to the edge of the bench. The salacious scenario was playing itself out faster than he wanted, but their fevered need had taken control.

"Count to three," he said, urgently stroking himself, "then rub yourself again and come for me!"

"One—" she began breathlessly, "two—three."

He thought he heard a muttered *thank you*, but he couldn't be sure and he didn't really care. Staring at her crimson backside and watching her fingers tantalize her clit, his cock was already begging to burst.

She suddenly gasped and threw back her head.

"Keith...ooh...Keith..."

Her bleating cry hurtled him into a shuddering climax.

Exploding over her red, curvaceous ass, sparkling wave after sparkling wave crackled through his limbs. He was catching his breath and trying to still his pounding heart when he heard her wails. Panting and slightly giddy, he slid to the floor just as her last spasm subsided. Cradling her into his arms, her body fell limp against him.

* * *

Quite minutes ticked by.

"I guess we should make a move," Keith murmured.

"I suppose," she said softly, shifting in his hold. "This isn't the most comfortable spot."

Slowly releasing her and helping her up, they stepped from the shower and he handed her a clean towel. Quickly drying off, she picked up the nightie she'd slept in.

"Carly, what were you thinkin'?" Keith exclaimed, staring at the lingerie in her hand.

"When?"

"When you decided to follow me down the hall in that nightgown?"

"I didn't have anything else, and I was thinking! I just had to be with you," she replied, gazing up at him. "After what happened in the storm last night, I, uh..."

"You didn't wanna waste a single second cos it might be your last?"

"Something like that," she mumbled, dropping her eyes and leaning against him.

As she moved her arms around his waist, he sensed the vulnerability she worked so hard to hide.

"Don't worry, baby," he murmured, then realized what he'd said.

He'd never called a woman *baby* in his life.

"I know it was a freak thing," she continued, "but I kept thinking, what if something like that happens again and I let this chance slip away? I had to follow you. I had to."

"Hey, I'm glad you did," he said softly, feeling a wave of fierce protection sweeping through his heart. "For the record, it was almost impossible for me to keep my hands off you last night, and even harder to leave you this mornin."

"I knew that when you climbed into bed with me, even though you kept that robe on," she remarked, pulling back and grinning up at him with a sassy smile. "When you left to come back here it was written all over your face."

"It was?"

"It was, otherwise I wouldn't have come after you."

He paused.

"What?" she pressed. "If there's something wrong—"

"No," he said sharply, then softened his voice. "Carly, I felt a connection the moment you walked in my office that first day."

"I did too. While I was at home getting ready to come back I thought about you constantly. When you almost fired me I was panic-stricken."

"And when I spanked you?"

"Uh...the truth is..." she began hesitantly.

"The truth is," he repeated, "it didn't turn you off, it turned you on, right?"

"Oh, my gosh, so much."

"I guess a hot backside isn't a deterrent after all!"

"But I was so embarrassed," she said hastily, "and the threat of a spanking is still a deterrent in a weird sort of way."

"But Carly, gettin' back to this mornin', weren't you in the least bit worried about runnin' into Andy or Elsie wearing that flimsy nightgown?"

"Andy was at the barn."

"What if he'd come back for some reason?"

"Highly unlikely."

"And Elsie?"

"I could hear her in the kitchen. She had the television on. I was a teensy bit worried, but not enough to stop me."

"Apparently," he remarked, raising one wicked eyebrow. "Carly Kincaid, you are a very brave, very bad girl."

"And you wouldn't want me any other way."

"True, but I can't have you runnin' back to the guest room in that nightgown. Put on my robe," he suggested, releasing her and lifting it off its hook.

"Oh, sure, that's way better," she declared, rolling her eyes. "Me prancing around in your bathrobe."

"What about your arm? That bandage is soaked. Speakin' of which, didn't it bother you?" he asked, then frowning, he added, "Dammit, I'm sorry, Carly, I didn't think about it."

"Neither did I. Does that answer your question?"

"I guess we both got carried away, but regardless, that wet dressin' needs to come off. I guess I need to speak to Elsie."

"I could tell her I took a shower."

"Nope, I'm not lyin' to her. I'm not sure how this is gonna play itself out, but she's gotta know what's happenin' between us."

"What do you mean, play itself out?"

"Things are complicated," he said evasively, his frown deepening.

"Uh, Keith, I know I'm not supposed to be nosey, but what is this for?" she asked, picking up a key hanging on a silver chain around his chest. "Does it open the door to Fort Knox? It must be important for you to wear around your neck all the time."

"Once upon a time it actually *was* the key to Fort Knox, but now I see it as a sort of talisman. That's all I can tell you."

"Maybe more later?"

"If you're a good girl," he replied with a grin, "and I hate to say it, but I've gotta call to make and some work to do. You'd best get your butt back into bed and I'll—"

"Back to bed? I don't need to go back to bed, I'm perfectly fine. Has the wind died down?"

"Most probably. Those winds come flyin' off the mountain overnight and they're usually gone by sun-up."

"In that case, what I need is some breakfast, then I have to see my poor truck," she said sadly. "I hope it isn't totally wrecked."

"I just had a thought. I have a track suit you can wear."

"How could you possibly have a track suit that would fit me?"

"The water in the washin' machine was too hot," he declared, taking her hand and leading her into the bedroom.

"You do your own laundry?"

"I was passin' the laundry room and I heard the machine goin'. I just tossed it in," he said, opening the bottom drawer of a tall dresser. "See if this fits."

Dropping the nightgown on the bed, she took the pants from his hand and pulled them on.

"Amazing," she declared. "I can't believe it. They're perfect."

"Try the top."

Carefully slipping into the thick, fleecy sweatshirt, she broke into a happy smile.

"This is amazing, and it's so warm."

"Great, but I don't have any socks. Never mind, Elsie will."

"Can we have breakfast now?"

"Sure, but I need to speak to Elsie alone first. You go back to the guest room and wait about ten minutes, then go down to the dinin' room. That'll give me time to talk to her, then I'll come back here and make the call."

"Okay, boss," she quipped, grinning up at him.

"I still am," he said firmly, though smiling back at her, "and don't you forget it."

"I wouldn't dare," she retorted as they headed to the door, but she abruptly stopped to stare at a large framed photograph on the wall.

"Is that this place?"

"That's how the ranch used to look. Kind of a mess. You're lookin' at the paddocks and barn. Over there is a photograph of this house taken from in front of the barn lookin' up."

"Keith, you've done so much. My gosh. How did you manage?"

"A great deal of hard work, but it's worth every sore muscle and every last penny. Come on, let's go. We both need to eat."

"I'll have to call my dad about Daisy," she said with a heavy sigh as they started down the hall.

"You have insurance, right?"

"Of course."

"So why is there a problem?"

"Neither of my parents wanted me in that truck, but I bought it anyway. Dad said Daisy was a death trap, and mom couldn't understand why I wanted to drive around in an old tin can that had a terrible heater and no air-conditioning. I admit there have been days I've agreed with her."

"Your truck is what I'd call a fun-mobile. A vehicle for fun, not every day use. Your dad was right. That windshield alone could've killed you. They don't shatter like that anymore."

"No doubt he'll remind me."

"We've got a sedan in the garage you're welcome to borrow if you need to."

"Thanks, Keith, but I have no plans to go anywhere."

"This is where you get off," he said, stopping at the guest room. "Check your watch. Ten minutes, got it?"

"Got it."

"You seem to like old things," he remarked, spying her battered Timex.

"Uh, not especially. I just never got around to buying myself anything better."

"Ten minutes," he reminded her, then pecking her on the cheek, he sauntered down the hall.

* * *

As she watched him, she thought he had the sexiest walk she'd ever seen. His strides were long, his arms swung easily at his sides, and his shoulders were straight and square. As he turned the corner and disappeared, she let out a happy sigh.

"What I wouldn't give to be a fly on that wall," she said wistfully. "I wonder what you'll say about me, and what will Elsie think?"

Her fingers were wrapped around the bedroom door handle.

She was pushing it down.

Then she wasn't.

CHAPTER EIGHT

Carly wasn't sure why she was refusing to listen to her voice of reason. She knew she should have slipped into the guest room, waited ten minutes just as Keith had asked, then ambled down to the kitchen. Instead she was walking silently down the hall.

Promising herself she'd only listen for a minute or two, she paused deciding which direction to take. She could enter the dining room and listen through the door that led to the kitchen, or eavesdrop through the kitchen door itself. Thinking there'd be less chance of discovery in the dining room, she was about to enter when she heard Keith and Elsie talking.

Startled, she abruptly stopped.

Heart thumping, she prayed they wouldn't come out and find her.

"Why am I doing this?" she mumbled under her breath. "I must be crazy."

But she knew the answer.

It wasn't just because she wanted to hear what Keith said about her.

That was more the excuse than the motive.

It was the secrecy surrounding him and the ranch.

"You make the best coffee, Elsie," she heard Keith remark, "but you know that."

"Keith, you haven't asked me to sit down with you to discuss my coffee."

"True..."

"I'm going to make this easy for you," Elsie continued, lowering her voice. "I know you've been with Carly."

"How could you possibly...? Oh, you checked on her."

"I did, early this morning, and there you were snuggled up together."

"Elsie, I have real feelin's for this girl," Keith said earnestly. "You know I wouldn't have let that happen if I didn't."

69

"This isn't news, Keith. I told you early on that you'd taken a liking to her, and you have my blessing, but you already know that."

"I can't hide this from the guys. I'll tell them later, but that's not the issue."

"No," Elsie said solemnly, "that's not the issue."

Carly's pulse ticked up.

"You're probably feeling you should tell her who you are, but you just met and anything could happen. That father of yours will do whatever he must to get you back to Houston. If he learns about this place he'll find a way to shut it down, mark my words."

"Why is he so damn stubborn? He's known since I was a boy my dream was to have my own horse ranch."

"Why are *you* so damn stubborn?" she retorted. "That's what he'd say."

"He has, many times."

"He's determined you'll take over the company, and you can't blame him. You inherited his gift for business."

"Will he ever let me be my own man and live my life?"

"If your mother was still alive there'd be a chance, but he's become obsessed with crowning you King and placing you on the throne. His business is his legacy, and Keith, you know how much he's changed."

"He sure has. What the hell is wrong with him?"

"He's my brother, but I can never forgive him for what he did."

"I know you're talkin' about Gary, but I still don't believe he was behind that whole thing."

"No-one beats your father, and Gary did. That oil lease was worth a great deal of money, and after your father lost, he was determined to get even."

"I'm sorry Elsie, but plantin' drugs in his house? Makin' an anonymous call and gettin' him arrested? That's not dad's style."

"Someone did it. Gary wouldn't even take an aspirin. He was totally railroaded, and Harlan was his only enemy."

"That you know of."

"Gary would have told me if someone else was out to get him."

"What about that horrible ex-husband of yours?"

"He was long gone. I don't even know where that bastard is, and it was a couple years after our divorce that I met Gary." Then lowering her voice, she wistfully added, "I'd waited to be with someone like him my whole life, and just when we were about to get married..." but she was unable to continue as the painful memory swept over her.

"I know you loved Gary very much. Still do."

"Of course I do, but your father knew that too, and he killed two birds with one stone. He set Gary up, and made sure he was sent to prison. But Harlan didn't just ruin Gary's life, he ruined mine right along with it, and I'm sure he thinks I deserved it."

"Because you were going to marry his competitor? I don't buy it," Keith said with a frown. "He knows you can't choose who you fall in love with. Mom's parents were against their marriage, and he had to fight to make it happen. Do you really believe he'd rip apart your love life? His only sister?"

"You and I have talked about this too often and too much. As I've said many times, Harlan was hopping mad when he lost that lease to Gary, and someone went to a great deal of trouble to make sure he was taken away from me."

"Maybe someone was making sure you were taken away from him."

"Same difference. When God took Mabel from your father, he turned angry at the world."

"Yep, he did," Keith grimaced. "Home was a bad place to be."

"She was his rock and his shelter, and the fact that I'm a nurse didn't help. The medical profession was one of the targets of his fury. I suspect he's become even more embittered. If he finds me here helping you, God help us both."

"You don't have to worry. My lawyer is a master at coverin' tracks, and so am I. Keith Parker doesn't exist, and I sure don't look like a businessman in a three-piece suit and tie when I'm here, not that I let anyone see me anyway. As far as the world is concerned, Andy Chapman is the owner and trainer of Dream Horse Ranch. Besides, Houston is halfway across the country."

"All I'm saying is, don't take any unnecessary chances. You can't say anything to Carly until you're one-hundred percent sure this girl can be trusted with your life, because that's what we're talking about, Keith, your life."

"All our lives. I care about her, a lot! I know that sounds crazy after such a short amount of time, but I do."

"You don't have to explain yourself to me. From the moment I met Gary he haunted me every minute I wasn't with him. He still does."

"Thanks, Elsie. I feel bad about keepin' up the pretense, but you're right. I have no choice. I just pray she'll understand when the time comes and I tell her."

"I hope that day comes sooner rather than later for all of us," Elsie said with a heavy sigh.

"I have to get to my office," Keith declared, rising to his feet. "I missed a conference call this mornin'. Dad will be as mad as a rattler in a sack."

"You'll talk your way through the drama, you always do. I'm just amazed there are phones that show a telephone number making it seem you're somewhere you're not."

"That's not the phone. I use an app."

"An app. I still don't understand what that means and I don't need to. I'm just glad you have something that works."

"Elsie, don't give up hope. Gary will be up for parole in just a couple of weeks. God willin' you'll have your life back."

"I swear, every minute away from that man has felt like a lifetime. I miss him so much. I'm just praying your father doesn't interfere. He knows some powerful people."

"I'm sure he'll be too busy with other things. Try not to worry. I'm off to make that call, but I'll be back to join Carly for breakfast."

"How is she? Better I assume."

"Not as much as I think she's pretending to be, and her arm needs a fresh bandage. She should be here any—"

A light knock interrupted him. Turning around, he saw Carly poking her head around the door.

"Is it okay to come in?"

"Great timin'," Keith declared. "I was just leavin' to make that call I told you about. I shouldn't be long."

"Hello, Carly," Elsie said warmly. "You'd better let me take a look at that arm. Are you hungry? What would you like for breakfast?"

"I don't want to be any trouble."

"Trouble? Goodness, it's no trouble, it's my job, but first sit down and have some coffee while I fetch my medical bag."

Keith was about to leave the room, but as Elsie disappeared into the kitchen Carly glanced up and sent him a wink.

"I won't be long," he said, winking back.

Feeling buoyed, he started down the hallway towards his office. Elsie had been right. His father was angry at the world, but Keith's job with his father's company was imperative, and would remain so for a few more months.

Keith had started Dream Horse ranch with an inheritance left by his mother, but he'd still needed to borrow. The land was in the perfect location and the acreage ideal, but the house, the arenas, the barn, and the outbuildings, had been run down. The ranch was profitable, but every penny went to the debt. He didn't want to break free of Boyd Holdings until it was paid off and he had capital in the bank.

Entering his office and settling behind his desk, he reached for his cellphone. Opening an app that would offer a false number and location, he placed the call.

"What the hell?" Harlan bellowed as he answered. "Where were you?"

"I'm truly sorry, and I don't blame you for being angry," Keith apologized, feigning remorse. "I'm not gonna give you some cockamamy excuse. I'll tell you exactly what happened."

"Go on then, let me hear it."

"I met a woman a while back, and over the last few days I've been spendin' some time with her. Last night she was in a real bad car accident. She was almost killed."

"Damn!"

"She was trapped in her vehicle, and I was one of the people who helped get her out."

"What? Are you okay? Were you in the car?"

"No, but I was nearby. Long story short, she's in the same hotel as me and after the paramedics looked her over, I walked her to her room. She was extremely upset and I ended up stayin'. I couldn't leave her by herself. It was probably about three o'clock in the mornin' when I finally closed my eyes, and I slept right through my alarm."

"I see. Sounds like quite the drama. How was she trapped?"

"A piece of lumber slid off the back of a truck and smashed through her windshield. She was in a vintage vehicle, so glass was everywhere. It's a miracle she survived. Her arm is scraped up and badly bruised, but otherwise she came out of it unscathed."

"Damn," Harlan repeated. "Well, son, I'm glad she's okay."

"Dad, we never know about things. It could've been me drivin' behind that truck."

"Don't even think it."

"Just sayin'...anyway, I am sorry I missed the call. How did it go?"

"Fine, fine, but I need you to listen."

"I always do."

"I mean really listen. I know you like working while you travel around and see this great country of ours, and I have no complaints about your productivity. Your reports are always in on time, you have great relationships with our satellite offices, but I need you here, in the office next to mine. The time has come for you to put your wandering lifestyle behind you."

"Why now?"

"Why *not* now?"

"You just said yourself you have no complaints. What's that old sayin'? If it ain't broke don't fix it."

"Why must you sound like a hick? The word has i-n-g at the end of it. *Saying,* not *sayin'.* I didn't pay for a first-class education for you to sound like some small-town cowboy."

"I've met a lotta folks in small towns and they're good honest people. A whole lot more honest and good-hearted than most of the people we deal with."

"Talking that way came from that damnable stable you used to hang around," Harlan continued, not responding to his son's comment. "Being with all those horse handlers was a bad influence on you. I should have stopped it before it began."

"Why didn't you?"

Keith heard his father take a breath.

He knew the question would stop the badgering.

Harlan had allowed him to hang out at the local western barns because his wife, the woman he'd cherished and adored, had insisted upon it. She'd said their son was never happier than when he was around horses, and everyone at the stable said he had a natural gift.

"We're digressing," Harlan said brusquely. "Like I said, I need you back here."

Keith paused.

"Okay. I'll move my trip up," Keith said, thinking it might be wise to put in an appearance earlier than he'd planned. "I'll come in a couple of days, rather than next week."

"You will? That's great. We'll go to Vic and Anthony's for a steak."

"My mouth's waterin.'"

"Watering!"

"That too," Keith retorted with a chuckle. "See you soon."

Dropping the phone on his desk, Keith leaned back, let out a heavy breath and closed his eyes. His father's constant nagging and living a double life was exhausting, but Keith believed the end result would be worth the effort. Now he'd met a sexy young woman who not only shared his passion for horses, but his love of kink to boot.

As the thought floated through his mind, he smiled.

He couldn't wait to uncover the depth of her dark, decadent desires.

CHAPTER NINE

Carly was determined to check on Winston and see her much-loved truck to view the damage. But while Keith thought it was a good idea, Elsie disagreed.

"Trust me, in a little while you're going to be so tired you won't be able to stand up," she warned. "I think you're pushing your luck. You need to rest."

"But I feel absolutely fine."

"What about your arm?" Elsie asked solemnly. "Don't tell me that doesn't hurt."

"Sure, but I've competed with worse injuries," Carly declared, then hastily added, "Sorry, I know you're only watching out for me."

"If you must go, please be careful," Elsie said firmly, "and I'm not just talking about your injury. A trauma like the one you've been through can catch up with you."

"I'll keep my eye on her," Keith promised, rising from the table. "Come on, Carly. I know you're itchin' to see Winston and that pickup of yours. We'll take the golf cart."

Walking from the dining room to the foyer, he opened the front door, and Carly stepped outside. Puffy clouds floated across a powder blue sky and the air was cool, but not cold. Though the perfect day belied the horrific overnight winds, debris was scattered everywhere.

"What a mess," she muttered. "It will take forever to clean this up."

"Andy will arrange for a crew to come in," Keith assured her, taking her hand and leading her to a small shed. "There are part-time laborers around here who do odd jobs and take care of situations like this."

"I'm amazed we didn't lose power."

"That's not somethin' I worry about. We have generators, but you're right. The power lines are often ripped off their poles during wind events."

Climbing into the golf cart, they started down the driveway, but when they turned down the gentle slope towards the cabin, Carly grabbed Keith's arm.

"Oh, my God! How the hell did I walk away from that?"

"Damn. And I thought it looked bad last night," he muttered.

"Keith, I'm feeling weird."

"I'm not surprised. I can't believe what I'm seein'."

"It looks so much worse than I thought it would."

"I'll drop you at the cabin. While you're gettin' changed I'll take some pictures for your insurance company. When are you gonna tell your folks?"

"If my mother sees a photo of this she'll be catatonic for days, and I'm not sure dad will be much better. I'm their only child. They're extremely protective."

"I know what you mean."

"You're an only child too?"

"Uh, yeah."

"Sorry, that question just slipped out," she said hastily. "I wasn't prying."

"No problem," he said, shooting her a wink. "I'll wait until that branch has been removed, then take some pictures just for them. It won't look quite as bad."

"Thank you. They can't see that log through the windshield."

"Carly, we're lookin' at a miracle," he said solemnly. "You had an angel on you're shoulder, that's for sure."

"I can still see the moment in my head, but...uh...Keith..."

"What is it?"

"I'm dying to tell you this, but you have to promise you won't think I'm crazy."

"Did something else happen?"

"Sort of."

"Dammit, girl, you're killin'' me! What?"

"You said there was an angel on my shoulder," she began softly. "Keith, I saw the branch coming and suddenly I literally couldn't move. Someone—something—well—uh—shoved me down and held me there. That's how the log missed me."

"Damn," he grunted, a dark frown crossing his brow. "Maybe you just froze in fright."

"There's more, but you'll think I'm losing my mind."

"Take a deep breath and tell me."

"Okay, here goes nothing," she mumbled, staring at her hands. "After the branch had crashed through the windshield, a voice whispered in my ear, and before you say anything, it wasn't the wind."

He didn't respond.

Lifting her eyes, she saw his frown growing deeper.

"I knew you'd think I was crazy," she mumbled. "Maybe it was—"

"Carly, can you describe the voice?" he asked, cutting her off.

"It was a woman. She said, *trust him,* and your face flashed in my head."

* * *

Keith placed his fingers against his chest to feel his key.

What Carly had told him—surely it was impossible.

Or was it?

But as he put his arm around her shoulders, a light breeze swirled around them.

A warm chill pricked his skin.

"So, uh, do you believe me," she asked hesitantly, "or do you think I was imagining things?"

"If you heard a voice, then you heard a voice," he murmured. "Did it scare you?"

"No, just the opposite. I was panic-stricken, but her voice helped me. I swear I felt a presence watching over me."

"Watchin' over you..." Keith repeated, his voice barely a whisper.

Carly thought she heard his voice crack, but abruptly pulling back, he smiled down at her.

"You're alive because of a miracle," he declared. "That's what matters."

"Thank you, Keith."

"For what?"

"Everything, and for being so open about what I just told you."

"There are more things in heaven and Earth, Horatio, than are dreamt of in your philosophy. One of Shakespeare's greatest lines."

"A cowboy quoting Shakespeare?"

"What can I say? I was forced into a literature class when I went to college. Are you ready to go down to the cabin?"

"Sure, but now I have a thousand new questions rolling through my head, and I know I can't ask one of them."

"You'll get some answers at some point," he promised, moving the golf cart slowly forward.

But a minute later he came to an abrupt stop. The carport had been severely damaged.

"Dammit. The whole thing is about to fall down," he said, staring at the roof off its frame, and the supporting beams leaning at a sharp angle.

"Oh, no!" she exclaimed. "I need to get changed. Can I even get to the front door?"

"Nope. Use the bedroom door in the back."

"But it's locked from the inside."

"Then I'll go in through the front and open it up."

"This is unbelievable," Carly said as they climbed from the cart. "Will it take long to fix?"

"That depends," he replied solemnly. "Hopefully Salvo and Andy can do it. Gettin' a contractor here will take time."

As she started around the side of the cabin, Keith moved closer and studied the damage. Though the wreckage appeared stable, he didn't waste any time walking to the front door. But he wasn't prepared for what he found when he opened it. A window had been blown out. Broken glass, magazines and busted photo frames littered the room.

Stepping carefully around the havoc, he cautiously entered the bedroom. To his great relief it was untouched. Moving quickly to unbolt the back door, he found Carly waiting on the patio. It was still in once piece, but staring up at him with a pained expression, she shook her head.

"I walked by the broken window and saw the mess inside. Thank God I wasn't home. I guess I was lucky twice."

"I guess you were," he muttered with a sigh, taking her into his arms. "Did you have anything valuable in there?"

"No, thank goodness. I'm only half way through my unpacking. What now?"

"Here's the really bad news," he said gravely, cupping her chin. "Looks like you'll be stayin' in my house, eatin' Elsie's cookin', and sleepin' in my bed."

"Oh, no! That is terrible news!" she exclaimed in mock horror. "Surely there's somewhere else I can go? What about one of the stalls? Winston would love to have me in the barn."

"That sounds like a plan. Salvo can fetch you a winter blanket from storage. You'll be real comfy under one of those."

"Will you visit me?"

"I'd better not. I'd have to blindfold all the horses. God forbid they see me spankin' your ass or—"

"Stop!" she exclaimed, unable to suppress her smile a second longer. "The image of all the horses blindfolded..." but breaking into a giggle she was unable to finish.

Keith grinned, but not because it was a funny thought. He'd wanted to distract her from the carnage and he'd succeeded.

"Enough of this," he said with a chuckle. "I'll take photographs of your truck while you get changed and pack up your stuff."

"Okay."

"I'll put you in the guest room closest to mine."

"Why the pretense?"

"It's not about a pretense. You'll need closet space, but more importantly, when you've been a bad girl I can spank you and send you to your room."

"I'll never be that bad," she said, shooting him a wink.

"Uh, Carly, I guess this as good a time as any to tell you...I'll be takin' off in a couple of days, but I won't be gone long."

"Bummer."

"Yeah, but when I come back I'll have some surprises for you."

"Really? What sort of surprises?"

"That would be tellin'," he said, then dropping his lips to her ear he whispered, "but I'm gonna need them bein' around a naughty girl like you."

"Ooh, Keith, you just made me all weak."

"There's nothin' I'd like better than to take you into that bedroom and ravage you," he murmured, pulling back, "but I'll bet dollars to donuts Andy and Salvo will be here any time now."

"They will?"

"Yep, so, young lady, you'd best take your wobbly legs inside. I'll leave the golf cart. You can drive it back up to your truck."

"Okay," she said with a sigh. "You make a compelling argument, but let it be noted that I leave your arms under protest."

* * *

As Keith turned and strode away, Carly walked inside and flopped on the bed. There was a warm flood between her legs, and a deep yearning coursing through her body. The traumatic events of the night before had been terrifying. Shuddering as the drama flashed through her head, she let out a long sigh, laid back and closed her eyes.

"Keith, we wouldn't be together now if that hadn't happened," she mumbled. "I wouldn't have been in your shower this morning. Betsy might be a write-off, talk about a silver lining...!"

* * *

Walking up to Carly's truck, Keith spied Andy and Salvo rolling to a stop in the mule. A chainsaw and other tools were visible in the back.

"Hey, Keith," Andy said, jumping out. "This pick up looks worse than it did last night."

"No kiddin'," Keith agreed, watching Salvo approach the wreckage and study the embedded log. "I've gotta take some pictures, then you can start workin' on it."

"Removing that branch will be rough," Salvo declared. "There's glass everywhere."

"If you can't, don't sweat it. Just cut it down," Keith suggested. "I don't think the tow truck will care if there's a stump stuck in the window. Oh, and don't forget to empty the glove box."

"Sure thing," Salvo replied. "How's Carly?"

"Good, considerin' everything she went through last night. She's packin' up a few clothes. Andy, will you come with me and check out the damage?"

"Sure," he said, falling in step beside Keith as they ambled towards the cabin. "I assume Carly will be movin' up to the house."

"Yep, and about that..."

"Let me guess. You and Carly—you're kinda together."

"Yep."

"Hey, Keith, you know how I feel. I'm cool, just—"

"I know, just don't tell her too much too soon. The other thing is, I've moved up my trip. Dad's havin' one of his fits."

"Seems like he's been callin' you back more often."

"He is, and he's startin' to make me nervous. This place is still a few months off from bein' outta debt, and he's gettin' impatient."

"Time flies. We'll get there," Andy said confidently, "but if you need to spend more time with him to keep things on an even keel, you should. I can manage."

"I know you can, but you know when I'm away from this place I'm itchin' to get back. Now Carly and I are kinda, well, together, it'll be even harder. Speakin' of Carly, she's already talkin' about gettin' on her horse. I'm worried about her usin' that arm, but I know how she feels."

"Why don't you take her on one of the shorter trails? That would be an easy ride."

"That's a good idea. If we stick to the arena she might be inclined to show me some of her fancy moves."

"Here she comes," Andy said, seeing her approach in the golf cart. "Looks like she's got the suitcases in the back."

"Dammit. What was she thinkin' loadin' those in there?"

"You're gonna have your hands full. Good luck stoppin' her if she gets her mind set on somethin'."

"She's a smart girl. She'll figure it out."

"Figure what out?"

"This is my ranch, my rules."

"And your secrets."

"Yeah, and my secrets."

CHAPTER TEN

Carly was thrilled at the suggestion of the trail ride, and knowing she was eager to see Winston, Keith had dropped her off at the barn before driving the golf cart up to the house to unload her suitcases.

"You need to take care of that arm. Don't tack up," he'd warned. "I'll put the saddles on both the horses when I come back down."

She'd promised she wouldn't, but he knew she was a tester, and after putting her bags in the guest room, he was grinning as he left the house and jumped back in the cart.

"I'm gonna walk in and find both horses ready to go," he muttered to himself as he rolled down the gentle hill, but when he marched into the barn he found both horses waiting in the cross-ties, and Carly sitting on a bale of hay.

"I can't believe you actually did as I said."

"Of course. Why wouldn't I?"

"Need I remind you about a certain unexpected visitor who stepped into my shower this morning?"

"Did you tell me not to join you?"

"Smart-ass. I can see I'm going to have my work cut out for me."

"What work? What are you talking about?"

"You know what I think?"

"I'm not psychic, so no, I don't. What do you think, Keith Parker?"

"I think I'd better get these horses saddled," he replied with a wink. "Are you still feelin' okay? Not tired yet?"

"Do I look or sound tired?"

"Never mind," he said, shaking his head and striding past her into the tack room.

She couldn't help but giggle, and when he reappeared with the saddle for Pinocchio, she walked over to the cross ties to join him.

"Need any help?" she asked sweetly.

"Nope," he muttered, hoisting the saddle onto the horse's back.

"Are you sure?"

"Seems like the only person who needs somethin' around here is you."

"And what would that something be?"

"I'm sure you know the answer to that question," he said, turning to face her.

"Hmmm, let me think. What do I need? I know! A sexy cowboy who's a real good kisser. Any ideas?"

"I think you might run into that guy on the trail, but you'd better be careful."

"Because?"

"He loves spankin' sassy girls, and you've got one heck of a sassy mouth on you."

"But sassy mouths are the best ones to kiss. Doesn't he know that?"

"I reckon he does," he said with a chuckle, "but her lips get kissed after her tail gets spanked. If a sassy girl wants the pleasure she's gotta take the pain."

"Why?"

"Why? Why do you think?"

"I have no idea."

"Then I have a suggestion. When you run into that sexy cowboy who's a real good kisser, offer him some of your smart-ass remarks. He'll spank you hard and kiss you good, then he'll explain it."

"I'd rather he spanked me good and kissed me hard."

"You don't have a say in it. Now step aside so I can get that other saddle, or you're likely to be ridin' on a hot seat."

"I don't need the saddle, but thanks anyway, and if I wanted to push my luck I would say something like—I could think of worse things than riding on a hot seat."

"You're amazingly cheery considerin' your classic truck is wrecked and you didn't get much sleep."

"Now that you mention it, I do feel full of energy," she murmured thoughtfully. "I suppose that is a bit strange, but there's something else that brightened me up."

"What's that?"

"When you left me in the cabin it occurred to me if the windstorm hadn't happened and that branch hadn't plowed through my windshield, I wouldn't have ended up in your house last night, and we wouldn't have, uh, you know..."

"Made wild passionate love in the shower this mornin'?"

"Yeah, that."

"Fate can be a funny thing," he said lowering his voice, "and that was the best start I've had to my day in a very long time."

Suddenly placing his hands on either side of her face, he leaned in and pressed his lips on hers in a warm, languid, tender kiss.

"Mmm, I think I just found that sexy cowboy who's a good kisser."

"And I think sassy mouths are the best ones to kiss," he purred. "You're right about that windstorm. We'd still be dancin' around each other. Life is full of twists and turns. You've just gotta learn how to ride 'em, kinda like a horse. Sometimes the ride's smooth and easy, other times the goin' gets rough and you can hit the dirt."

"Yeah, I agree," she said softly. "Fall off and you need to get back on, but sometimes that's hard. Sometimes you just want to crawl into bed and stay there. I don't feel like that now, but last night trapped under that log, if I hadn't heard that whisper..."

As her voice trailed off his arms came around her, and closing her eyes she sank into his hold. The smell of the horses tickled her nostrils, she could hear them breathing, and Keith's heart thumped against her cheek. A deep sense of intimacy swept over her, and she felt as if they'd been together for years.

"So, Carly," he said softly, "you wanna ride with me?"

"Try and stop me!"

* * *

Carly had expected Keith to take her across the back fields and up the mountain, but he surprised her, leading her into a heavily wooded area not far from the barn. As they neared the trees, the debris from the storm grew thicker, and Keith pulled Pinocchio to a stop.

"I'm thinkin' we might have had a twister," he remarked. "I've never seen it this bad."

"Are you worried about going in?"

"Not at all. The visibility is good, and there's a trail that leads to a meadow next to a pond."

"That sounds great. Let's do it."

"Your horse sure is a calm guy. New place, all this crap around, and he's not battin' an eye."

"Winston's my big brave hero," she said, leaning over his neck and petting him.

"I still can't believe you ride him in a halter."

"Sometimes I just use a rope around his neck."

"Amazin'. Okay, follow me. You'll find the trail narrow when we go in, but it opens up and you'll be able to ride alongside me."

Relaxed and happy, he moved his horse into the thicket, but as he rode through the shards of sunlight piercing the overhead canopy of crisscrossing branches, Carly's startling admission, *someone—something—shoved me,* flashed through his mind, and so did his mother's passing.

When she'd been in the last stages of her illness, his father had arranged for her to be brought home. There was an endless parade of nurses and physicians, friends and relatives, but one afternoon she had asked to be alone with her son.

"Sweetheart, go into my closet and find my red coat," she said, looking at Keith earnestly.

"The one you wear to church?"

"Yes, that's the one. Inside the pocket you'll find a key."

He'd found the coat and retrieved a small key on a long chain. When he returned, she'd told him to put it over his head.

"Keep that around your neck and don't take it off until you're ready to use it. That's the key to your future," she'd said solemnly, taking his hand and gripping it tightly. "Go to the Hanover Bank and ask for Miriam. She's one of the managers. Inside the safety deposit box is cash, stock certificates, and information about an account. You're the beneficiary. Sweetheart, I know your dream is to own a horse ranch, and that's my dream for you too. What I've managed to put away should be enough to get you started. Your father knows nothing about this and he never can. He'd feel betrayed, and I don't want to hurt him."

"Mom...I don't know what to say."

"If I was going to be around I could help you break away from the company, but that's not going to happen. I'm sad to say your father will never understand who you are. He'll fight to keep you next to him, but you'd be miserable sitting behind a desk. You were born with a passion for horses, and you must follow your dreams. This is your life, not his, and you must live it."

Sitting on his horse and ambling through the trees, Keith could feel the heat in his throat as the memories flooded through him. It was his mother who had introduced him to horses. His father had no problem with his wife spending time at the local stable. It made her happy, and if she was happy he was too. She had quickly realized her son had inherited her deep love for the noble animals, and enrolled him in a lesson program. Andy Chapman, the newest and youngest trainer, had taken him under his wing.

But it was something else his mother had said that haunted him. She had leaned towards him and placed her painfully thin hand on the side of his face.

"I don't know what lies beyond this earthly plane," she'd said pensively, "but if there is another existence, I'll be watching over you. I'll help you find your dream ranch, and when you meet that special girl, I'll watch over her too. You remember that, and if something strange happens, something you can't explain, believe that I'm there doing what I can to help you. Do you promise?"

"Yes, mom, of course I promise."

It had been a stammered reply. He'd been awash with sorrow, and as he remembered the moment his eyes filled with tears, but the trail opened up and he could hear Carly moving up beside him.

Someone—something—shoved me.

"Thank you, mom," he whispered. "Thank you for saving her."

As the words left his lips, Carly appeared at his side, and they were suddenly moving through a ray of bright light.

Lifting his gaze he saw the wide break in the overhead branches.

"I'm so glad you brought me to this gorgeous place," Carly said softly. "I thought you were going to take me up the mountain."

"I changed my mind at the last minute," he muttered, trying to control the quiver in his voice.

"I'm glad. Sometimes things are meant to be."

Taking a deep breath he turned and faced her.

The rhinestones on the comb in her hair were sparkling, and the silver buttons on her shirt were reflecting the sun's bright light.

"Yeah," he murmured, "there's no question about it. Some things are just meant to be."

CHAPTER ELEVEN

As the meadow opened up before them, Carly thought she could have been walking into an oil painting. Daisies freckled the lush green grass, bulbous clouds dotted the baby blue sky, and the paddock, shaped in a perfect half-moon, encircled a calm sparkling watering hole.

"Keith, this place is a dream."

"Yeah. I come here all the time."

"I'll bet you do."

Sliding off her horse, she quickly removed his halter, and Keith watched with a worried frown as the big grey wandered off and began grazing.

"Are you sure you wanna do that?"

"Do what?"

"Let him loose," he replied, climbing down from his saddle. "I know you can ride him bareback in a halter, but aren't you worried he'll go wanderin' off?"

"Heavens no. Why would any horse leave this incredible grass? Besides, he'd never leave me. If I started walking back through the woods he'd follow."

"Seriously?"

"Would you like to see?"

"Yeah, actually, I would."

As she let out a whistle and began walking slowly away, Winston picked up his head and moved briskly towards her.

"I can't believe my eyes," Keith muttered. "That's incredible."

"I've changed my mind, big fella," she said, patting Winston on the neck as he stopped at her side. "We're going to stick around a while."

"Okay, Carly, I'm convinced."

"If you took that saddle and bridle off Pinocchio he'd stay here too."

"How can you know that?"

"Like I said, no horse would walk away from this incredible grass, but besides that, he won't leave Winston."

"They might fight."

"Winston won't fight, and I watched Pinocchio at the fence line. They're friends already. Did you see any issues between them when we were walking together?"

"No, but this goes against everything I was taught—and believe for that matter."

"If you're uncomfortable, tie him up."

Keith studied Winston peacefully grazing, then looked at Pinocchio. His horse had never given him any trouble. Still not convinced, but hoping Carly was right, he began unbuckling the girth.

"Andy will have my hide if he hears about this," Keith muttered. "You're absolutely sure he won't wander off."

"Would you leave a dining table in a high-end restaurant with a perfectly cooked steak in front of you?"

"Okay, here goes nothin'. I can't believe I'm doin' this."

Leaning the saddle against a tree trunk, Keith slipped off the bridle. The horse licked his lips, looked around, ambled towards Winston, then dropped his head to graze.

"You see?" Carly grinned. "No problem."

"My poor heart is hammerin'."

"Take a deep breath. Everything is fine."

"Yeah," he murmured, walking over to her. "This is about as fine as it gets. The horses are naked. How about we join them?"

He slid off her jacket and dropped it to the ground, then lifted her T-shirt over her head and unsnapped her bra. As he tossed it aside, Carly unbuttoned his shirt, but before she could finish stripping it away, he kneeled down and pulled her into the soft grass. Straddling her body, he hastily pulled it off, then put his lips to her ear.

"Ever made love outside?"

"No, and I feel so naked."

"You'll feel even more naked in a minute."

He finished undressing her, then stood up and stripped, gazing down at the gorgeous sight in front of him. The sun bathed her in its warm bright light, and her nipples had puckered from the air's soft touch. Wanting to capture the vision and lock it in his memory, he traveled his eyes across her body, taking in every detail.

Carly watched him for a moment, then closed her eyes. The cool breeze tickled her skin, the smell of grass and pine wafted around her, and she felt amazingly, gloriously free. She sensed him kneel beside her, and as his fingertips feathered the inside of her thighs, his mouth pressed against her lips. A moment later his fingers slipped into her sex, and though there was nothing demanding in his attention, he was sweeping her away.

Unlike their urgent coupling in the shower, Keith took his time. She moaned softly, reacting to the slightest touch, and he used her utterances of pleasure to guide him in his journey. Moving his mouth from her lips to her cherry tips, he drew them in and gently sucked. His fingers had found her wet and ready, but he didn't thrust them inside her hungry channel, focusing instead on her clit. He twirled and agitated as he continued to nibble her nipples, continuing until she was lifting her pelvis and gasping her plea for more.

"I want you," she bleated. "I want you even more than I did this morning."

"Please tell me you're on birth control."

"I am, and I'm safe, I swear."

"Me too."

Kneeling between her legs, he pulled her into his pelvis, rested his cock at her entrance, slowly snaked inside, then grabbed her waist and slowly pumped.

"Harder, faster," she begged, "please."

"Not yet."

As she let out a frustrated groan, he lowered himself down, and staying buried inside her, he rested his weight on her body.

"Keith, you feel—"

Her words were cut off by his lips pressing against hers, and as his tongue explored her mouth, she wriggled urgently beneath him.

"No, no, babe," he purred, moving his mouth to her ear. "I'm in no hurry."

To her great dismay, she felt him pull out, but as he kissed his way down her body, her disappointment transformed into joy. Diving his head between her legs his tongue frolicked against her clit, bringing her to the edge, then backing off until she was pleading for her release.

"Are you ready for my cock?" he growled, flipping her over.

"Yes, yes, please, Sir."

Grasping her hips and pulling them up, he plunged inside her, and thrusting with quick strong strokes, he could feel her nearing her climax, but he slowed, closing his eyes to relish the feel of her tight, pulsing pussy.

"Please, please, I can't stand it!"

Gazing down at her perfect backside, he landed several sharp slaps, but the sting fueled her burning hunger and she squirmed against him. Gently pushing her on to her stomach, he rested on her body, moved his legs outside hers, and pushed them together. He felt deliciously clamped, and as he began to thrust again, the sensations sent the blood rushing to his loins. Grabbing her wrists he stretched her arms above her head and held them down.

"Now I'm going to fuck you really hard."

On the edge for so long, Carly thought she'd explode from his wicked whispered promise, and when his cock began slamming into her, she knew there would be no stopping the eruption. Not this time. Not if he paused, or even if he pulled out. His pelvis grazed her bottom with every stroke, she was pinned by the weight of his body and his hands gripping her wrists. He was possessing her, and as the massive orgasmic balloon reached the bursting point, she squeezed her eyes shut and held her breath.

The explosion rippled through her limbs.

Shooting stars rocketed through her brain, and wave after wave of dazzling sensations washed through her body. Through the violent paroxysms of pleasure, his mouth consumed her neck, and he spoke wicked words in her ear. Every time she thought the spasms were waning, his cock continued to plunder her pussy, sending her back into euphoria.

Then suddenly it stopped.

He was rolling off her and she wrapped up in his powerful arms.

The world was still.

She was at peace, and deliriously happy.

* * *

A cool breeze whistled around them.

Carly snuggled closer.

Stirring from his doze and opening his eyes, Keith saw a slate grey ceiling in place of the white cotton clouds. It was late in the day and the weather was changing. His eyes scanned the meadow for the horses. They were side-by-side gnawing each other's withers, joyous in their mutual massage.

"What time is it?" Carly asked, yawning as she shivered in his arms. "Man, I feel totally wiped out, and cold, really cold."

"Because it is cold," he replied, reaching for her T-shirt and jacket. "Here, put these on. We need to leave. I think some rain is comin' in. This time of year the weather is unpredictable."

They finished dressing, but as Carly turned to whistle at Winston, Keith grabbed her hand.

"Hey, come here," he said softly, wrapping her up. "I'm not much good at, uh, talkin' about how I feel, but you're becomin' real special to me."

"I feel the same, and I'll never forget today, not ever."

Her voice had been a tremulous whisper, and leaning in, he softly drifted his lips over hers, then brought her back into his arms for a long, tight hug.

"Neither will I, and I'm gonna hold you all night."

"Yes, please."

They started across the paddock, and when she whistled and Winston began walking towards her, Pinocchio stayed with him.

"If that isn't the damnedest thing," he said, shaking his head. "I thought Andy was a horse-whisperer, but you've got him beat."

"I wouldn't say that, I've watched him and he's incredible. I think we're on the same page, but your horses are worth a ton of money so he's cautious. He has to be."

"You think?"

"Yeah, sure," she said with a nod as she looped the halter over Winston's head. "Andy doesn't want to take risks no matter how small, and in his position that's the smart thing to do."

"I've known him a long time, and you're right, he's a smart guy."

Leading Winston to a nearby tree trunk, she used it as a mounting block and jumped on his back, then waited as Keith tacked up Pinocchio. Placing his foot in the stirrup, he swung himself into the saddle, and they started into the trees.

"Keith, Elsie was right."

"What about?"

"I am starting to feel a bit funny, and not because of what we just did."

"Funny how?"

"As if someone knocked the wind out of me. It doesn't make any sense, not when I've just woken up from a nap."

"When we get back to the barn, take the golf cart up to the house."

"Maybe you're right."

"Are you okay to ride back?"

"Uh-huh. What I'm doing isn't riding, I'm just sitting up here."

He could see her face was pale, and he chided himself for making love to her. She had seemed fine.

"Keith, it wasn't that," she said as if reading his mind, "and even if it was, I'd do it all over again."

"What about your arm."

"Sore, but no big deal."

The remainder of the ride was quiet, and finally reaching the barn, they climbed off their horses and led them inside. Both Andy and Salvo were there, and as Carly took Winston to his stall and slipped off his halter, Andy walked up to help Keith.

"Give me Pinocchio," Andy said, taking the reins from Keith. "You need to get Carly home. She's white as a ghost."

"You noticed?"

"Hard not to. I'll call Sandy and see if she can come in tomorrow."

"That's a great idea. Thanks, Andy. I'll see you at dinner."

"One thing," Salvo said, walking up to join them. "I got the branch out of the pickup, but when I saw those dark clouds rolling in I covered it with a tarp. I know the truck is all smashed up, but a classic is still a classic. Anyway, here's the stuff from the glove box."

"Thanks, Salvo," Keith said, taking the plastic bag, "and I'm glad it's protected. Good thinking."

Walking down the barn aisle, Keith found Carly leaning up against Winston's stall.

"Let's get up to the house. You need a lie down."

"Yes, please. I feel like I'm going to pass out."

With an arm around her shoulder he walked her out to the golf cart, and as they started up the gentle slope, Salvo stood at the barn door and watched them.

"She probably shouldn't have taken that ride," Andy remarked as he joined him.

"Yeah, she didn't look too good," Salvo muttered. "Hey, Andy, I don't mean to speak out of turn, but, uh, are they a couple now?"

"Why do you ask?"

"Because if they're not, they should be."

"Yeah, they are," Andy said with a grin, "and Keith was fixin' to tell you."

"It's none of my business, but I'm glad. They look right together."

* * *

The moment Carly climbed into Keith's bed, she fell fast asleep. A short time later over dinner, Elsie suggested she was suffering from delayed shock.

"I didn't want her going out," she declared, "but that is one stubborn girl."

In spite of the circumstances, Elsie's comment sent visions of Carly naked and shackled swirling through Keith's head. After the meal, Keith hurried into his office and visited his favorite BDSM website.

He often used Andy's credit card to buy items online, and Andy was happy to oblige. Keith had made it possible for him to leave the chaos of the large show barn in Houston to head up his own operation. While Andy was a brilliant horseman, he didn't have a head for business. That was Keith's forte. The close friends had forged the perfect partnership.

With the order placed, Keith settled into his backlog of work for Boyd Holdings. The hours ticked by, and finally shutting down his computer, he meandered down the hall to his bedroom.

Staring down at Carly asleep in his bed, he felt his heart swell. Quickly peeling off his clothes, he slipped between the sheets and snuggled next to her warm body.

Closing his eyes, he breathed her in.

She was under his skin.

It was both thrilling and worrisome.

But he promised himself to focus only on the joy.
He'd worried about too much for too long.
As his eyelids grew heavy, she stirred next to him.
Softly cradling her, he let his fatigue sweep him away.
An angel watched over them.
Everything would work out just as it should.

CHAPTER TWELVE

Early the following morning Keith was woken by the salacious sensation of Carly's fingers around his very stiff member. Lying on his back, she was snuggled against him with her head in the crook of his shoulder.

"Whatta ya doin'?" he grunted groggily. "Why aren't you sleepin'?"

"I think you know what I'm doing, and if your bedside clock is right I've already slept a ridiculous number of hours."

"Because you needed to."

"Apparently, but now I need this."

Pushing back the covers, she rose up over him, held his member against her entrance, and slowly lowered herself down. Gazing up at her full breasts topped with pink puckered nipples, and her dark hair spilling around her creamy shoulders, the word Goddess sprang to mind. She looked breathtakingly beautiful. Gripping her waist and holding her still, he sent his cock upward with a powerful thrust. Throwing back her head, she let out a cry, followed by another and another each time he drove his manhood home.

"Please lay me down and fuck me?" she suddenly mewled. "I want to be taken, totally taken."

Wishing he had all day and a bag full of wicked toys, he artfully maneuvered her on her back, then locked his fingers through hers and held her down.

"Are you sure you're okay?"

"I feel great. Better than great."

"Ready to be ridden?"

"So ready."

"Gallopin' all the way? I'm not gonna draw this out."

"God yes, if it pleases you, Sir."

"Good answer."

Pumping with quick forceful strokes, he didn't stop until they were both at the brink, then abruptly paused.

"Why...?" she bleated, wriggling beneath him.

"Because I can."

He'd lowered his head down and breathed the teasing words in her ear. Moving his lips to her neck, he sucked in her skin, then kissed his way down to her breasts and nipped her nipples.

"You ready for more?" he finally asked, lifting his eyes to meet hers.

"Yes, yes, but please will you let me come this time?"

"Are you gonna be a good girl?"

"So good, I swear."

Slowly thrusting, he gradually accelerated, pumping with quick, strong strokes before backing off once again.

"I thought you said you weren't going to draw this out," she groaned. "Please let me come."

Vigorously driving his cock inside her, he continued until her eyes squeezed shut and she sucked in a deep breath.

She was on the edge.

"I'm counting to five," he growled. "You come on five and not a second sooner."

Her response was a strange bleating sound, and as he began to count, each number coinciding with his inward stroke, he could feel his own climax looming. Suddenly letting out a euphoric wail she writhed beneath him, but with his climax still building he continued to pummel her pussy. His eruption was abrupt and violent, and he could hear his deep groans uniting with her waning wails. Moments later, completely drained, he collapsed next to her and rolled on his back.

"I'm not sure we should have done that," he panted. "You're still—"

"I'm still nothing," she protested breathlessly, and reaching for the covers she pulled them up and nestled against him. "I told you I feel great. You worry too much."

"That's my job," he mumbled, closing his eyes and pulling her next to him.

He felt at peace.

Carly made him laugh, she felt good in his arms, and he loved sleeping next to her warm, luscious body. In spite of Andy's cautionary words and Elsie's warning, he knew it wouldn't be long before he'd tell her who he was and the saga that was his life.

"You have to promise me to take it easy today," he said softly. "We don't want any relapses."

"I feel one-hundred percent normal and I need to ride."

"Well, young lady, Andy has arranged for Sandy to come in, so you're off the hook today."

"I didn't say I want to ride, I said I need to ride. I'll go crazy sitting around doing nothing."

"You thought you were okay yesterday and look what happened."

"Yesterday was yesterday, and I slept for ages. All I need now is a good breakfast. I'm fine, look at me," she exclaimed, abruptly sitting up. "Do I look like I'm about to pass out?"

"Damn, you're stubborn."

"Only when I'm right."

"Only when you're right?" he repeated with a chuckle, grabbing her and pulling her back into his arms. "I'm gonna steal that line. You may be fine now, but you may not be fine in an hour, or two hours, or later today. That's the point."

"Talk about being stubborn," she said brusquely. "I've got nothing on you."

"Don't be takin' that tone with me. Someone's gotta watch out for you, and in case you haven't figured it out, that someone is me."

"How about this? I'll only ride two horses and Sandy can take the others."

"Uhh..."

"I promise if I feel wobbly after the first one I'll give up the second. That's reasonable, isn't it?"

"We'll go down to breakfast, let Elsie check you out, and if she says okay, then okay, but only if you promise to keep your promise."

"I will," she said with a laugh. "I promise to keep my promise. That's hilarious."

"I'll be comin' down to the barn to keep my eye on you, and now that I think about it, I have an idea."

"Which is?"

"If Elsie gives her okay, I'd like you to sit on Domino."

"Wait. I'm confused. Isn't Domino one of the horses Andy's going to be showing to the buyers coming in?"

"He is, but one of those buyers is a woman. Connie Masters. She might wanna see another girl ride the horse before she gets on. It happened the last time she was here and Sandy wasn't prepared."

"Have you talked to Andy about this?"

"Not Domino specifically, but we discussed the idea in general terms. You ridin' so he can spend more time talkin' to the clients. He didn't think Sandy was good enough, but from what we saw on your videos, Andy and I believe you are."

"Really? Wow. I'd love to. That was my job for Max King at Circle K. Do you know him?"

"I know of him, but Andy's the guy who deals with all that stuff."

"Oh, right, I forgot. You're the phantom cowboy."

"Behave."

"I'm speaking the truth."

"For the moment," he said, then kissing her quickly, he slipped from the bed. "I'll talk to Andy. If he's good with it then—"

"Then, yay!" she exclaimed.

"I'm jumpin' in the shower, and no, you can't join me. I need to get movin', and I have to stop in my office before I head into breakfast."

* * *

As he disappeared into the bathroom and closed the door, Carly snuggled under the covers and smiled. Things were working out far better than she'd expected, but she was more intrigued than ever. From the conversation she'd overheard, his father would try to shut down the ranch if he learned about it, but was that any reason for Keith not to tell her more about himself?

Then there was Elsie and her story. The love of her life was in prison. Talk about drama.

"I can help you, Elsie, but I need more than just a first name, and asking questions will only get me in trouble. Seems like I only have one option. I'm going to have to have a poke around. I just have to make sure I don't get caught."

* * *

A short time later, as Carly hungrily devoured scrambled eggs, cooked tomatoes, bacon and toast, she persuaded Elsie she was well enough to get on a horse.

"But if you start to feel tired you need to sit down, and if the weakness lingers, come back up to the house. You don't understand how trauma can affect you, but I know about these things. Yesterday afternoon took you by surprise, right?"

"Totally. I felt as though a giant vacuum had sucked all the energy out of me, and I felt sick to my stomach. All I wanted to do was sleep."

"Learn from that, and don't push your luck."

"I'll bet this is Andy," Keith declared as the sound of his phone interrupted the conversation. "Yep. I'll take this in the kitchen."

As Keith disappeared through the swinging door, Carly finished her breakfast, washing it down with the last of her coffee.

"That was delicious. Thank you, Elsie, you've been amazing. Every-one has. I've never been at a barn like this. I'm used to a grumpy trainer telling me to suck it up and get back on."

"My only experience in the horse world is this place, but if we don't take care of each other we won't have much of a team."

"I love that, and there might be a way I can do something for you as well."

"Being sensible and not overdoing is all I want."

"Excuse me for interruptin'," Keith said as he reappeared, "but we'd best get down there. Andy wants to see you on Domino, and if it turns out you can only ride one horse let's make it count."

"Great, but I've got way more than two horses in me," Carly said, rising from the table, then hastily added, "but don't worry, Elsie, if I don't feel right I'll stop."

Leaving the dining room, Carly smiled happily. She couldn't wait to ride, and as she walked outside, she found the sun shining in a clear blue sky.

"This is going to be a really good day," she remarked. "I can feel it. Shall we walk down?"

"I need to take the cart. Andy said some laborers will be comin' to clear up the mess from the windstorm. When they show up I need to get back here pronto."

"This is driving me crazy," she muttered as they headed into the small shed. "What's your big secret?"

Before the words had even left her lips, she wanted to breathe them back in.

He was climbing into the cart.

She glanced up to gauge his reaction.

His lips were pursed.

His eyes narrowed.

He remained silent.

Unnerved and wishing she'd kept her mouth shut, she climbed in and took hold of the bar above her head. She was glad she did. Driving out of the shed, he headed down the driveway at a fast clip. As they neared the barn she spotted Sandy's car parked in the trailer area, and a moment later she ran out to meet them.

"Carly, how are you? I saw Daisy and the carport and cabin. Holy crap! I can't believe it. Are you okay?"

"I'm fine, honestly."

"You have to tell me everything."

"I will when we finish riding."

"Domino is all tacked up and ready," Sandy continued as they walked into the barn. "I can't wait to watch you on him. I've only ridden him a few times, but that was before Andy started working with him. Hi, Keith," she added, turning around and sending him a smile. "Sorry, I didn't mean to ignore you."

"No problem. I'm goin' up to the viewin' area."

"I'll join you in a few minutes," Andy said, stepping out of the cross ties. "I've just gotta give Carly some pointers on what makes this boy tick. Sandy, why don't you get Jezebel ready? You can give her a light hack when Carly's done."

"Sure thing."

* * *

Already striding to the staircase that led up to the balcony overlooking the arena, Keith's head was spinning. All he could think about was the short, sharp exchange with Carly.

What's the big secret?

Her words continued to echo through his head.

Taking the steps two at a time, he was sorry he hadn't whacked her ass on the spot. It had been a rude and thoughtless remark. When would she learn to respect his privacy?

"Seems like you've got another lesson comin'," he muttered, "and this time I'm gonna make damn sure I get my message across."

CHAPTER THIRTEEN

Keith could hear Andy climbing up the stairs. As he appeared and moved to sit next to him, Keith pulled an envelope from his pocket.

"Here," Keith said, handing it to him. "I did some personal shoppin'. The charge will appear on your statement as Gem Enterprises."

"Ah, thanks."

"Thank *you,* Andy. Things would've been a whole lot tougher without that card to hide behind. I don't know how I would've managed."

"And my life wouldn't be anything like this," Andy said solemnly. "I thank the good Lord every day that your mom brought you into the stable I was workin' at. What a three-ring circus that place was."

"Sometimes things are meant to be. Huh, that's the second time I've said that in the last few days."

"I reckon I'm lookin' at the first," Andy remarked as Carly rode into the ring.

"No comment," Keith said with a grin. "Damn, she looks good on a horse."

"Yep. That girl was born to sit in a saddle. Look at that."

"What?" Keith asked, leaning forward and studying her. "She looks great, but is there somethin' specific?"

"I don't mean her, I mean Domino. Look how relaxed he is. That was the first thing I was watchin' for. It took me hours to get him to chill under saddle. I didn't know how he'd react with a different rider, but he's doin' just fine."

"That's your trainin'."

"Only to a point. If Carly wasn't sendin' the right signals, he wouldn't be so mellow."

As Carly effortlessly moved the horse into the jog, quickened its pace, then graduated into a lope, Keith found himself struck by her graceful skill. Though the horse was changing speed and gaits, circling and diagonally crossing the ring, he couldn't see her cues.

"How does that happen?" he asked softly. "How can she get him to do all that without movin' her hands or legs?"

"She's kinda blown' me away too," Andy replied, almost mesmerized by what he was watching. "I was expectin' her to be good, but not this good."

"That doesn't tell me how she's making the horse move."

"You ever watch a horse race on TV?"

"Sure, plenty of times."

"If you raise your hand to block out the horses and just look at the jockeys, the top guys look like they're floatin'. They barely move."

"Huh. I never knew that."

"It doesn't matter whether you're jumpin' a fence or canterin' around a ring, the best riders make it look effortless. I guess that's true with any sport, but certain people can communicate with horses beyond technique. They get on and everything just works. I'm pretty sure Carly's one of those."

"But you are too."

"Sure. I have a way with horses, though I think the message I send is different to the one Carly puts out, but she's a woman. The energy wouldn't be the same."

"You want to see anything else?" she called, as she brought Domino to a slow halt.

"Damn, she didn't pull on the reins," Keith muttered.

"Magic," Andy chuckled. "Yeah, Carly. Let's see a gallop and roll back."

"Really? You'll let me do that?"

"Sure. You look great."

"I feel great, and he's amazing."

"Get ready, Keith," Andy said as she moved the horse forward. "I have a feelin' you're about to drop your jaw, and you know what else I just figured out?"

"What?"

"Carly doesn't know how good she is. That's part of why she's so effective. She lets the horse do the thinkin'. She's a guide, not a frickin' wrestler."

"Even so, are you sure you want her to do this? Connie's gonna be here tomorrow."

"If Connie sees what we just did, she'll be interested. But that's just the appetizer and she'll want the main course. Let's see if Carly can give it to her."

"What's the difference if you show Domino or if Carly does?"

"If she sees another woman ride him it'll clinch the deal."

"Because?"

"Connie will instinctively think, *if she can do it, I can too.* With a man in the saddle the perception changes. He can do it, but he's a guy. He's stronger than me."

"Ah. Right. That makes sense. I should talk to you more about this stuff."

"Yeah, you should," Andy said with a chuckle, "but you can keep all your figures and documents to yourself."

* * *

Sandy had finished tacking up Jezebel, but as she led the mare to the gate, she stopped short and stared at Carly in awe. The girl was as smooth as a lake on a windless day. Moments later, hearing Andy give her the instruction for a roll back, Sandy caught her breath. He had never let her take any of the horses into the tricky maneuver, especially not a horse that was about to be shown to buyers. It was a testament to the high regard Andy had for Carly, but it was also a trial by fire.

Sitting on the big-boned, handsome gelding, Carly was in seventh-heaven. The horse was push-button perfect, and she barely had to move a muscle to achieve the reaction she wanted. Less was more, but doing a gallop and roll back on a horse for the first time didn't always go as planned.

Her first trainer, an old cowboy named Monte who was more horse than human, had once told her to visualize everything she wanted the horse to do seconds before asking the horse to do it. He claimed if the rider pictured the action, not only would the horse see the image, the rider's body, hands and legs would automatically do what was needed. But she and Winston were so in tune she hadn't implemented Monte's sage advice for some time.

As she cantered around the ring mentally preparing herself for the challenge, Domino began to pick up speed. Normally she would use her legs to tell the horse to quicken its pace, and she had only imagined Domino accelerating.

The magic was already happening.

It was as if she was riding Winston.

She thought it, he did it.

That's how they had become such stars.

Did she have the same mystical connection to Domino?

The answer came as a sudden surge of energy rippled through her body.

Domino's energy.

He knew what they were going to do, and as he bolted into the center of the arena, she readied herself for the screeching halt.

Watching from the balcony, while Keith was holding his breath, Andy was filled with feverish anticipation, and the anxiety wasn't just about Domino and Connie Masters. If Carly had the talent and skill he believed she did, she would have a significant impact on the barn's success.

The dust flew, Domino slid to a stop, paused for a fleeting moment, then flawlessly pivoted and calmly cantered in the direction from which he'd come.

"I knew she'd pull that off," Andy exclaimed, slapping his leg and jumping from his seat. "WHOO HOO!"

"I didn't even see her lift a fuckin' rein," Keith mumbled. "How the hell...?"

"I love this horse!" Carly called as she cantered towards them. "He's awesome."

"He loves you," Andy yelled down at her, "and so do we. Take him on in," then turning to Keith he stared at him intently. "Do you know what you've done?"

"Me? What the hell have I done?"

"You've hired us a million-dollar rider. That girl could ride a frickin' donkey and make it look good. She's gonna take this barn up one heck of a notch."

"I, uh, I'm kinda speechless right now..."

"I'm goin' down to see how she's feelin'. If she's up to it, I want her on Preston. Damn. I can talk to the clients while she rides. We'll be unstoppable."

"Only if she's up to it," Keith said quickly. "Make sure."

"You wanna come down?"

"No, I need to sit here a spell. Just make sure she doesn't overdo it."

As Andy hurried away, Keith pulled the key from under his T-shirt. Holding it gently, he stared down at the arena.

Andy was right.

Carly was a million dollar rider.

It was fantastic.

But it made things even more complicated.

* * *

Walking into the barn aisle, Andy found Sandy hugging Carly and telling her how brilliant she was. Noticing Carly's hesitant response confirmed his earlier suspicion. She took her intuitive skill and talent for granted.

"But it wasn't me," Carly protested. "Domino is just like Winston. Easy as pie."

"Best get on with Jezebel," Andy said, wanting Sandy to be finished by the time Preston was tacked up and ready to go. "Like I said, Sandy, just an easy hack."

"Yep, sure boss," Sandy replied, "and Carly, I don't know about Winston, but Domino isn't that easy. You're that good."

"Carly, that was a real good ride," Andy said warmly as Sandy led Jezebel into the ring. "I'd like you to get on him for the buyers tomorrow. How would you feel about that? You'll get paid extra of course."

"That would be terrific. I'd love to, and thank you."

"How are you feelin'? Are you up to gettin' on another horse? Tell me the truth. I need you to be one-hundred percent tomorrow."

"I feel exhilarated, and yes, I can definitely ride another one. I can ride another three or four."

"One will be enough. I don't want Elsie yellin' at me," he said with a grin. "How would you feel about jumpin' on Preston?"

"The black beauty? I'd love to."

"He's got a different mindset. Preston needs to know you're up there. He needs more support."

"He sounds like a horse I used to ride called Kahlua."

"Say, what?" Andy exclaimed, staring at her in disbelief. "You rode Kahlua? Three times world champion Kahlua?"

"Just at the barn. I wasn't allowed to show him, but he was the same. He was insecure, but once he had confidence in the person on his back he was unreal."

"That's kinda how Preston is. He can get a bit jittery."

"I know exactly how to make him feel safe. Let's get him tacked up."

Keith had left the viewing area, and walking down the aisle he'd caught the tail end of the conversation. Andy was about to put Carly on the most difficult horse in the barn. He couldn't help but feel apprehensive.

"Hey, Carly," he called, walking towards them. "That was beautiful. Domino looked amazin'."

"I'm so excited. Andy just asked me if I'd ride him for the buyers tomorrow. Can you believe it?"

"I sure can. I just wanted to let you know I'm goin' up to the house."

"You don't want to watch me on Preston?"

"I sure do, but the laborers will be arrivin' any time now. I'll watch on the monitor in my office."

"How cool is that? Being able to look in on the barn whenever you want. I keep forgetting to ask for the login info so I can watch Winston."

"I'll give it to you when you come back up. Andy, are you and Sandy comin' up for lunch?"

"Sandy won't be stayin'. You can tell Elsie it'll just be the three of us."

"Will do. Again, great job, Carly. I'll see you in a bit."

Watching him leave, Carly sensed things weren't quite right, but she had no time to dwell on it. Andy was asking her to get Preston from his stall.

* * *

Elsie was in the laundry room when she heard the front door. Quickly dropping the clothes into the machine and adding the soap, she walked into the kitchen and found Keith pouring himself a mug of coffee. She knew immediately something was on his mind.

"Do you want to talk about it?"

"I sure do," he said solemnly. "Carly is, and I'm quotin' Andy, a million-dollar rider. He says she could ride a donkey and make it look good, and, drum roll...he's asked her to ride Domino for Connie Masters tomorrow."

"She's that good?"

"He's puttin' her on Preston as we speak, so yeah, she's that good. She's better than that good. She's the rider we've always wanted, but..."

"You don't have to say anything else. I know why you're worried. Keith, you're overthinking this. You get that from your mother."

"So you've said a hundred times."

"Because you need to be reminded. You're intimidated by Carly's talent and what she has to offer. You're suddenly afraid you might do or say something that will tick her off and might cause her to quit. Not only would you suffer, it would hurt the ranch."

"Exactly, and that's makin' me feel like I'm losin' control."

"Let's look at this from her perspective. Why did she decide to apply to be an exercise rider at a small barn in the middle of nowhere?"

"She said she was tired of bein' in the craziness of the city and the show barns there."

"Right. How hard do you think it would be to find another situation like this?"

"Uh, pretty damn hard."

"And now she's not just riding nice horses, she'll be showing them to potential clients. That's a really big deal for her. And let's not forget, she's crazy about you. If anyone's worried about keeping things sweet, that would be her. She has more to lose than you do."

"Elsie, I swear, if you weren't my aunt I'd marry you," he exclaimed, putting down his mug and hugging her. "Thank you."

"You're welcome, hon. Why don't you go into that office of yours and get to work? I'll make you some fresh coffee and bring it in with a muffin."

"Again, if you weren't my aunt..."

"Go on, out of my kitchen," she said with a warm smile. "I'll be there in a few minutes."

Letting out a grateful sigh, Keith walked through the dining room and headed down the hall.

"Elsie's right," he murmured under his breath. "Carly's gonna be an invaluable member of the team. It's up to me to keep her head on straight."

CHAPTER FOURTEEN

Settling behind his desk, Keith powered up his computer and switched to the live feed from the arena. Carly was walking Preston around the ring. She didn't appear to be as relaxed as she had on Domino, and when the horse suddenly tossed its head, she stopped and quickly climbed off. Andy hurried up to her, the two of them chatted for a minute, then led Preston out. Anxious to know the problem Keith picked up his phone and called Andy.

"Hey, Keith. I take it you're watchin'," Andy said as he answered the call.

"Yeah, of course. What happened?"

"Carly thinks Preston has a problem with his mouth and wants to ride him in a rope halter."

"Are you gonna let her?"

"I am. I think she might be right. The same thought crossed my mind the other day. Gotta go. I'll call you back when we're done. Keep watchin'."

Keith drummed his fingers impatiently, and just as he saw Carly enter the ring, Elsie arrived with his coffee and a muffin.

"Here you go," she said cheerily, placing the mug and plate on his desk.

"Perfect timin'. Carly's about to ride Preston in a halter."

"Is that a good idea?"

"We're about to find out. It was her suggestion and Andy's goin' along with it," Keith replied, turning the computer around so they could sit side-by-side and watch seated in the chairs in front of his desk.

"Isn't Preston the nervous horse?"

"Yep, and Carly thinks the problem is his mouth."

"What does that mean?"

"Probably his teeth."

Carly began by backing the horse up, turning it in a tight circle, backing up again, then walking off. A minute ticked by and she sent him into the slow jog. Keith could see the horse's demeanor had changed. His head was lower and he was clearly more relaxed.

"Would you look at that?" he muttered. "She was right."

"I'm no expert, but it sure looks good to me," Elsie declared.

"He's an impressive horse, but I've never seen him move like that," Keith continued. "He's floatin' across the ground."

Carly continued to move the horse through its paces, then brought him to a halt, jumped off, and led him back to Andy waiting at the gate.

"I'd say Andy was right," Elsie grinned, getting to her feet. "You've hired yourself a million-dollar rider. I'll make us a special dinner tonight to celebrate."

"How the hell am I gonna be able to concentrate on Boyd business with this happenin'?"

"Just remember pretty soon this will all be yours. Mabel would've been real proud of you, Keith. I'm sure she felt badly that she couldn't stash away enough for you to buy something outright."

"I have no complaints, Elsie. I could've found a smaller ranch, but I knew this was the right place even if it did mean borrowin'. There were too many coincidences that brought me here."

"Dream Horse Ranch," she sighed. "The ranch you always dreamed of and Mabel made possible."

"I told Carly it was because we sell people the horse of their dreams, and I guess that's true as well."

"I like that," Elsie smiled, "and I'll bet Mabel would have too. I'll see you at lunch."

Turning his computer around, he returned to sit behind his desk. It had been a remarkable set of circumstances that had led him to the rundown farm.

Carly's miraculous escape from death suddenly flashed through his head.

A shudder rippled through his body.

"Am I crazy thinkin' you saved her?" he mumbled, reaching under his shirt to touch the key.

But his phone rang, snapping him from the solemn moment. Glancing at the screen and seeing Andy's name, he snatched it up and answered the call.

"Tell me," Keith said urgently. "Obviously Carly was right, but I want the details."

"She's convinced Preston has been nervous because he has a bad tooth, and you saw the difference. I would never have put that horse in a halter like that, but dammit, she was right on the money."

"Are you callin' the doc?"

"Nope. She's recommended a horse dentist, a guy by the name of Steve Sampson."

"But we always use the vet."

"You're not gonna believe what she said to me."

"Do I want to hear this?"

"Yep. She said, *Andy, if you have a toothache do you go to your doctor or your dentist?* I didn't have an answer for that one, and when you think about it, it makes sense."

"How do we reach him?"

"She's puttin' a call into him right now. He travels all over."

"What do you suggest when the buyers come tomorrow?"

"I'll walk Preston out so they can see him close up, but I'm not lettin' anyone on his back 'til this is taken care of."

"What a mornin'," Keith muttered. "Is Carly still feelin' okay?"

"Seems to be. She's gettin' Winston out right now."

"To ride?"

"Nope, to take down to his paddock. We're finished here. Sandy's about to leave, and Carly and I will turn out the rest of the horses."

"I'll see you at lunch then."

"The workers are at the gate. Gotta go."

The call ended, and rising from his chair Keith stood at the window and stared down at the barn. Two trucks were rolling down the driveway, and Salvo was by the crumpled carport waiting to greet them.

A flash of white caught his attention.

Carly had left the barn with Winston beside her.

As she started the short walk towards the paddocks, he noticed Sandy climbing into her car. The only character missing was Andy, but Keith knew Andy would be in the barn fussing over Preston.

"Dammit, I wanna be down there. I wanna talk to the workers, I wanna be with Andy and checkin' on Preston, I wanna be leadin' those horses out myself. This is my life. I'm sick of hidin' out like some kinda criminal."

Turning around he stared at his desk. The thought of opening up spreadsheets and dealing with the business of Boyd Holdings was as appealing as jumping in a freezing pond in the middle of winter.

"I can't keep doin' this," he grunted angrily. "I've gotta bring things to a head. I need to start livin' my life. I'm a cowboy, dammit, not some pencil pushin', deal-makin', oil tycoon."

* * *

Elsie had suggested inviting Salvo to join them for lunch, something she did if there was reason to celebrate. Keith had agreed, but Salvo wanted to stay with the workers.

"Salvo is a loyal guy with a heart as big as the mountains, but he's not always comfortable in social situations," Keith said as they sat down at the table. "Sunday dinners are different. We talk about the barn so he sees it as part of his job."

"Is it okay to ask where he came from?" Carly asked cautiously. "He seems more urban than country."

"I guess there's no harm in it," Keith replied. "I was downtown walkin' to my car late one night and two guys jumped me. Salvo was sleepin' in a nearby alley and he threw himself into the fight. He was just a kid, but man, he was tough. You can see how he's built."

"I don't think I've ever seen anyone so muscled up," Carly replied. "He looks like a weightlifter."

"He is. That's his passion. Even back then he was powerfully built. I swear he saved my bacon. When I found out he was livin' on the street I started takin' care of him. I never asked how he got there. I figured if he wanted to tell me he would. He's mentioned bits and pieces, but I still don't know his story. When I got this place, I drove him out here one day and asked him if he'd like to work for me. He couldn't get here quick enough. In fact, he lived here before I did, renovating the cabins."

"My gosh. Poor Salvo, but lucky Salvo as well."

"I've been workin' at barns my whole life, and I've never met a guy who works as hard as that kid," Andy remarked. "I'll tell him to take a break, he smiles and says thanks, then keeps on goin'. But we should talk about tomorrow?"

The conversation turned to the wealthy clients. Though Carly paid close attention and offered her own ideas, she noticed Keith was unusually quiet. When the lunch came to an end, she caught him staring at her with an odd expression.

"Let's go clean that tack," Andy said, rising to his feet.

"Andy, I need a few minutes with Carly first," Keith said. "I won't keep her long."

"Not a problem, and Carly, if you hear from that horse dentist go ahead and make the appointment. Any time is fine, except tomorrow afternoon, of course, when the buyers will be here."

"Will do."

As Andy left, Keith asked Carly to join him in his office. He seemed tense, and when they entered and he locked the door, her butterflies burst to life.

"Take a seat," he said formally, perching himself on the edge of the desk. "First, I wanna tell you how impressed I am. You're not just a beautiful rider, you care in a way most people in this business don't. You didn't immediately think Preston was actin' up for no reason, you asked why. That's how I am. When a horse isn't behavin' right, I ask why. Is the saddle hurtin', is he tired? Whatever. That's what you did today, and that blew me away more than anything else."

"Keith...I don't know what to say, but you look so grim. I thought something was wrong."

"The way things are going with you and Andy I couldn't be happier."

"Then why are you so serious?"

"Before we went down to the barn you said somethin' that upset me. Carly, you knew better...so...I've gotta ask myself why?"

"Are you comparing me to a horse?"

"Horses can't speak. They can only communicate through their behavior. Humans can do both, like you did earlier."

"What did I say?"

"You can't think of anything? Are you sure about that?"

Suddenly recalling the moment in the shed, a hot flush crossed her cheeks.

"Sorry," she mumbled. "I shouldn't have said, *what's the big secret?*"

"It wasn't just what you said, it was the way you said it. How do you think that's been sittin' with me?"

"Uh, not good," she said softly, dropping her gaze and wishing her stomach would stop doing back-flips.

"Why did you say it?"

"It just sort of—came out."

"Not good enough."

She sighed, then shifted in her chair.

"Carly, just spit it out!"

"Okay. It pisses me off."

"What does?"

"That you won't tell me anything about yourself."

"But, Carly, you knew the situation here from day one. If I hadn't been straight with you, then sure, you'd have a reason to complain, but I did. You came into this with your eyes wide open."

"You're right, and I really am sorry," she said, hoping he'd accept her apology. "It won't happen again, I promise."

"The thing is," he continued, "things are gettin' a bit complicated."

"I don't understand."

"You're workin' for me and we're gettin' involved. We're gonna have some speed bumps, but whether I'm your boss or your boyfriend you've gotta remember this is my ranch, with my rules, and Carly, they're my secrets. Mine to tell when I deem fit. Repeat that, please."

"This is your ranch, your rules, and they're your secrets. Yours to tell when you deem fit."

"Have you got that through that head of yours now?"

"Yes, Keith," she replied, feeling like a scolded ten-year old.

"You were downright disrespectful. Do you remember what I said when I spanked you?"

"Uh, yes," she breathed, recalling his edict.

"Tell me."

"You said if I broke the rules again, if you didn't fire me, you'd take a strap to my backside."

"I sure as heck am not gonna fire you. Do you wanna quit?"

"No!" she exclaimed, darting her eyes up. "Not in a million years!"

"I told you what would happen, and I'm a man of my word. Is there anything you wanna say?"

"No, except, uh, I'm almost afraid to say this, but maybe there was a part of me that was, uh, testing the waters, but it won't happen again, I swear."

"Go over to that cabinet and open the top drawer. You'll find a strap in there. Bring it to me."

"Seriously?"

"Do you see me laughing?"

Silently cursing, she rose to her feet, but as she walked nervously across the room, excitement sent goosebumps popping on her skin, and slick moisture flooded her sex. She wanted to know how it felt. Wondering if there was something wrong with her, she picked up the black leather strap and carried it back to him.

"Can I tell you something?" she murmured softly. "It's kind of weird."

"You can tell me anything."

"I...uh...maybe later."

"That's fine too. Pull down your jeans and panties, leave them around your ankles, and place your hands on the desk."

Nervously she did as directed, but as he gripped her hips and pulled her back, she closed her eyes and sank into the feel of his fingers against her skin.

She wanted him.

She wanted to feel his cock inside her.

She wanted him to rip off her shirt and bra.

She wanted him to knead her breasts.

She wanted him to utterly devour her.

* * *

Keith was about to land some hot slaps in preparation for the strap when he spied her glistening dew.

She was wet.

The stern lecture—the pending punishment—the entire scene had made her hot.

His suspicions were confirmed.

She harbored dark fantasies.

The thought sent his cock surging to life.

For a fleeting moment he was tempted to forego the discipline and ravage her senseless, but she needed and wanted to be punished.

He wasn't going to let her down.

CHAPTER FIFTEEN

Carly wriggled impatiently.

The wait was driving her crazy.

But was that the point?

For interminable seconds Keith's hand had fondled her backside.

"You know why you're being punished, but it bears repeatin'," he suddenly declared, landing a hot slap. "You were rude, and you asked a question you knew was completely inappropriate. That's not tolerated at this ranch," he continued, raining his flattened palm on her blushing cheeks. "Rules are rules! I expect them to be followed! Do we understand each other?" he demanded, vanquishing any doubt she had about his resolve to punish her if he thought it necessary.

"Yes, Sir," she cried out hastily. "I'm sorry. Truly I am."

"Six with the strap. Three for each offense. Are you ready?"

"Yes, Sir."

The first strike hit the center of her backside eliciting a loud yelp. The second fell just below the first and she yelped again. When the third hit, she stared at him over her shoulder.

"I've learned my lesson," she bleated, "I swear. You're right, I was rude."

"Good. Three more and you're done. Ready?"

"Ooh, yes, Sir."

Delivering each blow beneath the one before it, he sent the last against her sit spot. As she stamped her foot and let out a howl, he began smoothing his hand across her hot skin. Though her bottom burned with a hot, prickling heat, her pussy was soaked and she craved his cock.

"Keith?" she whimpered, staring back at him with pleading eyes.

"Yeah, babe?"

"Maybe I shouldn't ask you this, but please will you make love to me?"

He hesitated, but fleetingly, then swiftly clutching a fistful of hair, he leaned over her body and planted his lips against hers in an endless, devouring kiss.

"Don't move," he breathed, finally pulling back.

She watched as he straightened up and hastily removed his belt. Quickly unzipping his jeans and letting them fall around his legs, he took hold of his member and presented it to her slick wetness. Closing her eyes, she was about to thrust back at him, when he clutched her hips and plunged inside her.

"I'm gonna fuck you 'til you come," he growled, "and I won't be stoppin'."

Whether it was his proclamation, his pelvis slapping against her stinging backside, or the urgency of his pummeling piston, Carly had no idea, but she was suddenly swept away in a vortex of thrilling erotic lust. Every nerve sparked, and her orgasm was building into a giant bubble ready to burst.

* * *

Carly's gasps and moans were growing in pitch and volume. There was an unexplainable urgency to their coupling, and as she curled her fingers into fists and released a piercing wail, he knew she'd been seized by her orgasm.

Slowing his strokes and closing his eyes, he relished the feel of her walls pulsing against him, then suddenly his climax shuddered through his body. The convulsions surged through him as he violently erupted inside her warm, moist depths, but they passed just as quickly, leaving him breathless with his heart pounding. As he slipped out and opened his eyes, he found her shuffling unsteadily, trying to turn around and fall against his chest.

"Are you okay," he managed, sucking in the air as he wrapped her up.

"I'm amazing," she replied, letting out a heavy breath. "Except for my sore ass."

He couldn't suppress a grin, then gently releasing her, he held her face between his hands and lovingly glided his lips over hers.

"There's a bathroom through that door," he murmured, pulling back and jerking his head across the room. "You go first. I'm sure Andy's wonderin' where you are."

"I'm sure he is," she mumbled, but took her time pulling up her jeans and moving away.

Zipping himself up and ambling across to the window, he gazed down at the workers. The carport had been broken down, and Salvo was helping load the wreckage into a truck while another group gathered up the scattered branches. The laborers were from south of the border or enthusiastic young cowboys, but spotting an older, light-haired man who seemed out of place, a vague chill pricked his skin.

"It's all yours."

Turning around, he watched Carly walk toward him, her face tinged pink and her eyes twinkling.

"You'd better get back to work," he said as she neared. "I hear the owner of this place is a real task master, and he spanks lazy girls."

"No! Seriously?" she quipped with a sassy grin.

"He does, and disrespectful, disobedient ones as well."

"I hear he takes a strap to their ass. Damn that must hurt."

"I reckon it does," he grinned, "but it's supposed to."

"Am I forgiven?" she asked, suddenly speaking softly and wrapping her arms around his neck.

"You're forgiven, but have you learned your lesson?"

"Absolutely, but, uh, I wanted to tell you before..."

"Yeah?"

"I love, uh, consequences."

"That's good, cos you can count on 'em. Now get your ass down to that barn."

"Yes, Sir, Mr. Boss man," she said with a wink, then pecked him on the cheek, pivoted on her toes, and headed to the door.

His heart full, he watched her leave, then returned to the window. The carport had been broken down, and the scattered debris was almost cleared away.

"Dammit, I should be down there," he muttered. "I'm done with this bullshit."

Grabbing his phone and opening an app, he used an unidentifiable number to call his father.

"Harlan Boyd."

"Hey, dad."

"How many phones do you own, son?"

"Just one at a time. I told you, I don't like those expensive smart phones. Lose one and you're screwed."

"I guess," his father said with a chuckle. "What's up?"

"Will you be in town this weekend?"

"Sure will, why?"

"I'm comin' in."

"Say, what? That's great. Nothing's wrong, is there?"

"Not really. I just need to talk in person."

"Sounds good. What time will you get here?"

"Not sure. I haven't booked a flight yet, but late mornin' if I can catch a red-eye."

"I'll see you when you get here. Looking forward to it."

Ending the call, Keith let out a breath. It was nerve-wracking, but he was already beginning to feel the relief that would come from ending his double life.

The sandy-haired man abruptly popped into his head.

Texting Salvo, he asked him to come to the office. Knowing it would take Salvo a couple of minutes to walk up to the house, Keith picked up his mug and empty plate, and carried them back to the kitchen.

"Thanks, Elsie, that hit the spot," Keith declared as he walked in. "Something smells good."

"Slow cooked steak stew," she replied, stirring a pot as she stood at the stove.

"My favorite."

"Yep."

"Elsie, I'm goin' to Houston tomorrow. I'll be leavin' early."

She paused, studying him, then placed the wooden spoon on the counter.

"You've got a look in your eye. Have you hit the wall?"

"Hittin' the wall is a good way to put it, and yeah. Elsie, I can't do this anymore. I wanna be down at the barn, I wanna meet the clients and hang out with the horses. I'm tired of runnin' in here like some guilty jackass every time someone pulls into the driveway. This is no way to live."

"I agree, but what are you going to do?"

"I'm close enough to weather the storm if dad cuts me off."

"That's quite a risk."

"I know you think he's a bad guy, and he can be ruthless in business, but I'm sorry, I still don't believe he screwed you and Gary. I just don't."

"That's a different discussion for another time," she said solemnly. "If you think it's time to tell Harlan about this place and what you've been doing, then you should. He'll have a meltdown, you know that, but maybe when he comes out the other side he'll surprise you."

"I'm not countin' on anything except his foot on my backside as I walk out the door."

"Keith," she said, softening her voice, "whatever happens we'll work things out, and speaking of doors, are you expecting anyone? I'm sure I just heard someone come in."

"Salvo. I wanna ask him about a worker. I got one of my bad vibes."

"If you're worried about some casual laborer recognizing you, you're right, you do need to talk to Harlan," she remarked. "Before you go, a package arrived for Andy. Would you mind taking it to his room?"

"No problem, and thanks, Elsie," he said, giving her a hug. "I couldn't have done any of this without you."

"Of course you could, and you saved me, remember? Estranged from Harlan and my man in prison for something he didn't do, I was at a complete loss. You gave me a new home. God knows where I'd be if you hadn't brought me here."

"Hey, if you hadn't joined me I'd be livin' on frozen dinners," he retorted with a grin. "We needed each other. We still do."

"You'll be having a frozen dinner tonight if I don't get back to my stew," she quipped, smiling back at him. "Go on, don't keep Salvo waiting. He's a busy young man."

"Yes, ma'am."

Leaving the kitchen and striding through the dining room into the hall, he spied Salvo waiting outside his office door.

"I'll be right there, Salvo. Go on in."

Salvo turned and waved.

Continuing into the foyer, Keith picked up the large parcel and grinned. It was from Gem Enterprises. His box of wicked toys. The day just got better. Carrying it down to his office, he walked in and placed it on the coffee table.

"Hey, Salvo. Thanks for comin' up so quick. Take a seat. It looks like you made quick work of that carport."

"I'm thinking we should use stronger joists on the roof. That wind could happen again."

"I agree. Go into town and get whatever you need."

"I will after the laborers leave. So, what do you need?"

"Maybe I'm being paranoid, but I noticed one of the guys is older, and he doesn't look like your everyday worker. Do you know anything about him?"

"I was worried when I saw him too," Salvo remarked, leaning forward in his chair. "I've never seen him before. Apparently he showed up about a year ago, but he comes and goes."

"Huh. What's your feelin'?"

"He seems okay, doesn't talk much, just goes about his job."

"Has he asked any questions?"

"Nope. Not one."

"That's good to hear, but keep your eye on him. I'll mention it to Andy as well, even though there's probably nothin' to it. By the way, I'm leavin' for Houston early in the mornin'. While you're here, is there anything you need to talk with me about?"

"Uh, no, except, I really like Carly. You two are a nice pair. Sorry, was that crossin' a line?"

"Hell, no, and thanks. I guess Andy filled you in."

"He did. Anyway, I'd better get back. I don't like leaving those workers unsupervised."

"That's why you're the best."

"Good luck with your trip."

"I'll take it, and I'll be lookin' forward to comin' back to a new carport. A strong one."

Salvo broke into a smile, then rose to his feet and strode from the room. As the door closed behind him, Keith picked up his phone and called Elsie.

"Hi, Keith. Do you need something?"

"That worker, I'm not feelin' good about him and I don't know why. Make sure you keep the door locked and be extra careful while I'm gone."

"I will, but try not to worry. You're not the only man in the house. Andy's here."

"I know, but do it anyway, okay?"

"Sure, Keith. Thanks for the heads-up."

Dropping his phone on his desk, Keith swiveled his chair around and stared down at the tall lanky worker.

"Dammit. Am I bein' ridiculous?" he muttered, feeling his gut churn. "Why am I gettin' such a bad vibe about that dude? Screw it. By this time tomorrow I can stop worryin' about bein' recognized."

* * *

The sandy-haired man knew eyes were on him. Salvo had been covertly watching him since he'd arrived, and twice the man had glanced up at the house and spotted a figure at the window.

It had been by sheer accident he'd seen Harlan Boyd's son at an airport. Able to book a seat on the same flight, he'd snapped it up. The kid could have been going anywhere, but the sandy-haired man had a hunch, and his hunches always paid off. Unfortunately it had been the dead of night when the plane had landed in Seattle. Though he'd been able to follow the kid's black truck for some time, the man had lost it as it sped through twisting-turning backroads.

But the man came away convinced the tycoon's son had a place somewhere in the rural area. His mother had been a horse nut, and her son had inherited the gene.

The determined man had begun the hunt, eliminating one property after another. When he'd found Dream Horse Ranch, he'd noted the high gates and surveillance cameras. Tight security for a ranch. Hanging around the small town, he'd found very few people knew much about the place, except the horse flesh was pricey. He'd considered posing as a buyer to gain access, but quickly dismissed the idea. What he knew about horses could be written on the back of a matchbook.

Researching the title, he'd learned it was owned by a company, but only one officer was listed. Andrew Chapman.

Then fate intervened.

A fierce windstorm had created havoc.

Casual laborers rolled into town looking for work. Loitering among them, he'd stood in the background, biding his time, hoping the name of the ranch would be mentioned and he could wangle a job. The hours ticked by with no luck. He was about to throw in the towel when a truck rolled up bearing the Dream Horse Ranch name. Leaping in the back with half-a-dozen others, he was soon being driven through the imposing gates.

Now he was on the grounds, but he'd only seen two men, neither of whom was Boyd's son. The home was large and rambling. The man needed to gain entry and have a poke around.

A half-smile curled the edges of his lips.

He'd find a way.

He always did.

CHAPTER SIXTEEN

As the sun began to set, and the casual laborers packed up to leave, Keith retrieved his binoculars. So far he'd only seen the man's blondish head and back, but as the workers collected their tools Keith finally got lucky. Looking through the field glasses, he noticed the stranger's hair was long and scraggly, and he had several days of beard. What stood out the most was the man's skinny physique and lack of skin color. He wasn't a man who worked outside.

Keith's pulse ticked up.

Focusing on the man's face, he seemed familiar.

Grabbing his phone, Keith placed a call to Andy.

"Hey, Keith. What's up?"

"That guy I told you about, I think I recognize him, I just can't be sure. Did he ring any bells with you?"

"No, but I'll go over and take a closer look. If I recognize him what should I do?"

"Call me, but hurry, they're gettin' ready to leave."

"On my way."

Holding up the binoculars to watch, Keith spied Andy leaving from the barn, but Carly had walked out with him. They parted company, Andy striding towards the carport, and Carly walking up to the house. Swinging the binoculars back towards the stranger, Keith found him turning to watch her.

Suddenly his face became clear.

He was strikingly familiar.

Lowering the glasses to observe the entire area, he saw Carly turn her head in the stranger's direction. She lingered her gaze for a minute, then quickened her pace.

Keith's phone rang, almost startling him.

Glancing down at the screen, he saw it was Andy.

"So?" Keith asked urgently as he answered.

"Never seen him before, but you're right, he looks outta place."

"Okay, thanks, Andy."

Ending the call, he watched the man jump into the back of the truck with the other workers. As it drove away, though Keith let out a relieved breath, the incident bothered him. Needing a distraction, he decided to turn his attention to something much more appealing. The box of wicked toys.

He'd spent an enjoyable hour going through the contents and selecting the items he wanted to use later that night, but he was faced with a problem. Finding a suitable hiding place where Elsie wouldn't stumble across them.

Then it hit him.

His truck! He was the only one who drove it.

He could transfer the salacious items into a bag and lock it in the hidden compartment behind the seat.

Picking up the box, he carried it into his bedroom and through to his walk-in closet. Setting it on the floor and lifting a sports bag from the top shelf, he put aside the items he intended to use that night, then transferred everything else, planning to take it with him when he left in the early hours the following morning.

"Keith? Are you in here?"

It was Carly.

Hurriedly zipping the bag closed, he hastily stuffed the salacious items he'd set aside into the bottom drawer of his dresser.

"I'm in my closet. I'll be right out."

"I'm jumping in the shower. Care to join me?"

"I'm tempted, but I'm saving my energy for later."

"That sounds intriguing."

Her voice came from directly behind him. Jumping up, he spun around and found her standing in the door.

"You shouldn't sneak up on a fella like that. You damn near gave me a heart attack."

"What were you doing on the floor?"

"Normally I'd say none of your beeswax, but..."

"But?" she asked, stepping towards him.

"I was hidin' a surprise."

"You were? What kind of surprise?"

"You'll find out. How's your gorgeous ass?"

"Keith!"

"It's a simple question," he murmured, taking her into his arms. "Answer me. How's your gorgeous ass?"

"Tender, thank you very much."

"You should thank me very much."

"For what?"

"For spankin' you and keepin' you straight, and not spankin' you harder."

"Thank you and thank you," she said softly. "Are you sure you don't want to join me?"

"I definitely want to join you, but like I said, I'm savin' my strength."

"Uh, Keith..." she muttered, a frown crossing her brow.

"What's wrong, Carly?"

"It's probably nothing, but there was a creepy blonde guy among the workers today. I'm only mentioning it because I know how security conscious you are. He seemed out of place, and when I came up to the house just now, he was staring at me."

"I know, I saw him. Salvo kept his eye on him, and Andy checked him out too. He didn't wander off anywhere, or do anything suspect, but yeah, there was something off about that guy. "

"He sure gave me the once over, and he was blatant about it," she declared. "To be honest, he kind of freaked me out."

"Asshole," Keith muttered. "I'll tell Salvo not to use him again."

"I wish you weren't going away."

"Me too, but put him out of your mind and concentrate on showin' the horses tomorrow. At least I won't be around to distract you."

"I'll miss you."

"I'll miss you too, babe, a whole lot, but I'll be back real quick."

"Is it okay for me to sleep in your bed while you're gone?"

"Hell, yeah," he replied, then softening his voice, he added, "I'm not real good at the soppy stuff, but that's our bed now, and I'm gonna enjoy thinkin' about you keepin' it warm while I'm gone."

"For a cowboy who's not good at the soppy stuff that wasn't half bad," she said with a smile, "and you just made this cowgirl very happy."

"But you'd better keep your promise not to snoop."

"I won't, I promise. I know you'll tell me your secrets when you're ready. I'm okay with it now, honestly."

"Good to hear. Now you'd best get in that shower. Elsie will be callin' us into dinner pretty soon."

"Keith?"

"Yeah, babe?"

"Thank you for everything. I love working here, and I love being with you."

"I love havin' you here," he purred. "Now scoot."

As she turned and headed into the bathroom, he was tempted to call her back and tell her everything, but stopped himself. The following day was too important. She needed to have her mind on showing the horses, not caught up in his drama-filled life. Walking out of the closet, he thought back to the happy days when his mother was alive, and his father had been a funny, loving man.

"What the hell happened to you?" Keith muttered, absently touching the key under his shirt. "Did grief eat you up so much it left you without a heart?"

An unexpected notion suddenly rolled through his head.

His father had always believed his son would take over the business, and Keith has been keeping the ranch a secret because he'd feared his father's wrath. At least, that's what he'd told himself. But was it because he didn't want to add to his father's pain?

"Maybe it's both," Keith muttered, anxiety coursing through him.

The conversation with his dad wouldn't be easy, but Elsie's diagnosis had been right. Keith had hit the wall.

* * *

Though Salvo had been invited to dinner to celebrate Carly's promotion, no-one expected him to walk through the door. When he did, Carly was deeply moved. He'd made the effort for her. They shared a unique connection. He was the one who had found her trapped in her truck and saved her life.

"Hi, Carly," he said shyly as Elsie handed him a glass of champagne. "I saw you ride today. You were fantastic. When you were on Preston using just that halter with the reins attached, I couldn't believe it."

"Thanks, Salvo, and thank you for coming tonight."

"I wanted to," he murmured. "I'm really happy you're here at Dream Horse."

Watching them from across the room, warmed Keith's heart.

"Here's to your ride tomorrow," Andy suddenly said, raising his glass. "I know Connie Masters will be blown away when she watches you ride Domino. I'm willin' to bet she'll write us a big fat check."

Everyone laughed and clinked glasses, then took their seats at the table. As the dinner progressed, a sense of camaraderie and closeness filled the room. The champagne flowed, and halfway through the meal Keith excused himself to fetch a second bottle from the kitchen. Retrieving it from the refrigerator, he gazed out the window. The ebony sky was crystal clear, and a glowing perigee moon sat low in the sky.

He smiled.

It was a magical night.

Ambling back to the dining room, he pushed open the door—but abruptly stopped and caught his breath.

Salvo, Andy and Carly were shrouded in a golden light.

Touching the key beneath his shirt, a sudden epiphany rolled through him.

Salvo was the little brother he never had.

Elsie had taken him under her wing as her own.

Andy was his rock.

Carly was his wife to be, and the mother of his unborn children.

They were his family, present and future.

Heat flooded his body.

His head began to spin.

He thought he was going to pass out.

"Keith? Why are you standing there like that? Are you all right?"

It was Carly's voice.

He suddenly realized his eyes had been closed.

Opening them, he stared down at the table.

Four happy but concerned, faces gazed up at him, and there was no golden glow.

"Keith?" Elsie said, rising to her feet.

"Sorry, sit down," he replied hastily. "I'm fine. I was just lost in thought for a minute."

Fighting a sudden rush of emotion, and swallowing the heat searing the back of his throat, he stepped forward and placed the bottle on the table.

"What had you so deep in thought?" Carly asked. "You were a million miles away."

"Uh, how grateful I am you're all here," he replied. "Salvo, I don't know what I'd do without you, Andy, you're an amazing trainer, Elsie, you're the voice of reason for all of us, and you keep us from starving," he added with a grin, then looking across at Carly, he said, "As for you, you're the rider I've been waiting for since I opened this place, and I'm so glad you agreed to work with us. Thank you all for being here. You made Dream Horse Ranch a dream come true."

"My goodness, I don't know where all that came from," Elsie remarked, beaming at him, "but there's nowhere I'd rather be, and I'm sure everyone feels the same. Now sit back down and finish your supper before it gets cold. Andy, would you please open the bottle?"

"Sure thing."

As Keith took his seat, his body still warm and his heart full, he was convinced he hadn't been dreaming. His mother had filled the room with her loving energy, and shown him his life's path. More importantly, the anxiety he'd held about confronting his father had evaporated.

CHAPTER SEVENTEEN

As the celebratory meal came to an end, Andy was the first to excuse himself. Saying there was something he needed to take care of in his office, Keith followed him out, and while Elsie cleared the table, Carly walked Salvo to the front door.

"Thanks again for coming tonight, Salvo," she said earnestly. "I know you don't really like the whole social thing, and it means a lot you were here to celebrate."

"Carly, I, uh..."

A faint blush crossed his face.

Reaching out, she softly touched his arm.

"Salvo? What is it?"

"I don't like to talk about myself...but...uh..."

"You're my hero. I might not even be here if you hadn't found me. You can tell me anything."

"I'm not very good at talking."

"Take your time."

"My sister," he said quietly. "You remind me of her."

"You have a sister?"

"Yeah, but I don't know where she is."

"Oh, no. Salvo, that's awful. Can you tell me what happened? You don't have to if you'd rather not."

"I want to, if that's okay."

"Of course it's okay."

"We were in foster care. It was horrible and we took off. We were being chased so we split up. That was the last time I saw her. I walked the streets for days and days looking for her. I don't know why I'm telling you this. No-one knows. Shit. Maybe I shouldn't have mentioned it. Sorry."

"Stop apologizing. I'm so pleased you did," she said softly, her heart breaking for him. "I can't believe you've been carrying such a heavy burden all this time. Will you let me help you?"

"I don't know how you can. She could be anywhere."

"What's her name?"

"Theresa."

"I know I'm not supposed to ask personal questions, but you can trust me, I promise. I assume this happened in Houston."

"Uh, yeah, but..."

"Honestly, no-one will know you've told me, I swear. What's your last name?"

"Cavalleri."

"Thank you. How old were you when this happened?"

"I was fourteen and she was two years older."

"You poor thing. I'm so sorry."

"Carly, you're so much like her. Beautiful and brave and...," but as his voice cracked, he dropped his eyes to the ground. "I need to go now."

"Wait," she said, grabbing his arm as he turned to leave. "I'm sure Keith will want to help."

"He's already done so much for me, and he needs to stay under the radar just like I did when he found me. My foster father was crazy. He would've killed me, and Theresa too, if he'd caught her."

"Miracles happen, and I have a feeling you'll be seeing your sister again. Just keep the faith. Why are you looking at me like that?"

"That's what she used to say. Keep the faith. She'd say that whenever things were really bad."

"Maybe there's an angel looking down on you, and she wants you to know your sister is okay," Carly said earnestly, touching his arm again.

"I feel that she is. I pray for her every night."

"Let's get some air," Carly said softly, knowing he was fighting tears.

Opening the door and stepping outside, they found the huge moon low in the sky directly in front of them.

"Wow, look at that, Salvo," she murmured, gently looping her arm through his.

For a moment she thought she'd made a mistake, but he suddenly turned and hugged her. Moving her arms around him as he clung to her desperately, she heard a stifled sob, and wondered how long it had been since he'd felt arms around him.

"Carly? Where are you?"

Keith's voice broke the moment.

"Thank you," Salvo whispered, abruptly pulling back.

His red-rimmed eyes held hers for a brief moment, before he strode off down the driveway.

"Is everything okay?" Keith asked, stepping outside and standing beside her.

"More than okay," she replied softly. "Look at that moon. This is a magical night."

"Yeah, it is. Come with me. I've got some magic of my own waitin'."

* * *

Following Keith into his bedroom, she stopped short and caught her breath. The only light came from the fireplace, the flaming logs sending flickering shadows across the walls, and bathing the bed in a golden glow.

"This is wonderful," she murmured, but as Keith continued to lead her forward, she spotted four black leather shackles, a blindfold, and a small dildo on the bedspread. The butterflies in her stomach burst to life.

"Have you ever been tied up?" he asked softly, wrapping his muscled arms around her.

"Only in my fantasies."

"Are you ready for them to become reality?"

"I was ready the moment I saw you," she replied, her eyes sparkling up at him.

"Good answer. And the blindfold?"

"God, yes."

"Two outta two," he grinned, reaching past her to pick it up.

Placing the soft black foam across her eyes and securing it behind her head, he dropped his lips to her ear.

"Now I'm gonna peel off your clothes, and you're not gonna move."

His whispered instruction made her toes curl, and as he unbuttoned her blouse, slipped it down her arms and tossed it aside, a warm shiver rippled through her body.

"Keith...I feel so weak," she whispered as he deftly unsnapped her bra and dropped it next to her shirt.

"I don't want you falling over," he muttered with a chuckle as he sat her on the edge of the bed.

Pulling off her boots and socks and laying her on her back, she gasped as he unexpectedly lowered his mouth and nibbled her nipples. But stopping as abruptly as he'd started, he slid off her jeans and panties. She was about to spread her legs when he rolled her over, lifted her hips, and stuffed a pillow under her pelvis.

"Don't move," he ordered, buckling the cuffs around her wrists. "You look incredibly beautiful," he murmured, linking them together at the small of her back.

"I do?" she whimpered as he spread her legs and secured them to the posts at the foot of the bed.

"Yes, you do," he said softly, brushing the hair from her face and kissing her cheek. "How do you feel?"

"Incredible," she managed. "I'm loving this even more than I thought I would."

"Did you see the small dildo?"

"Uh-huh."

"I'll be sliding it into your backside. When the time comes you need to relax. Will you do your best to stay calm and accept it?"

"I'll try," she whispered, and though initially mortified, she couldn't deny a perverse curiosity.

"Good girl. Are you ready for your ride?"

"Aren't I already on it?" she quipped, the retort leaving her lips before she could stop it.

"You're in no position to be such a smart-ass," he scolded, landing a solid slap on her upturned bottom, "unless you want this ass to be stinging and red."

She was about to say, *sounds good to me*, but thought better of it.

Sensing he'd walked away, she listened keenly. Hearing a familiar sound, she realized he'd returned with a glass of ice. Without warning a cube touched her back just below her shackled wrists, then moved across her backside. Squealing, then gasping, she let out a shocked cry as he pressed it against her pussy. But her wild wails quickly changed to moans of pleasure. Diving his mouth against her sex, he hungrily lapped the ice and tantalized her clit.

"Do you want me inside you?" he finally asked, raising his head.

"Please, please," she bleated. "I want you so much I can't stand it."

"Since you sound so desperate..."

Carly was overcome.

Spread apart, restrained and blindfolded, though exposed and vulnerable, she loved the sense of helplessness. The ice had been a startling surprise, and when it had touched her pussy she'd almost seen stars... but his mouth had sent her even further into a vortex of sizzling sensations. As he placed himself at her entrance and thrust forward, she knew there would be no stopping her looming orgasm. His fingers digging into her skin, he began pumping with slow, powerful strokes, then slowly accelerating, he slipped his finger between her pussy folds and rubbed her swollen, sensitive nub.

She sucked in the air.

Her body grew taut.

He quickened his pace.

"Keith...Keith..."

It was all she could manage as her orgasm swept her up and sent her into delicious, dizzying spasms.

* * *

Expecting Carly's explosive convulsions, Keith continued to ride her until she shrilled her last cry, and her body fell limp beneath him. Carefully pulling out, he stretched out alongside her, and pressed his lips against hers in a languid, loving kiss.

"What about you?" she murmured, feeling his hard cock against her leg.

"What about me?"

"You didn't climax."

"That was only round one, baby."

"Round one?" she whimpered. "How many rounds are there?"

"Seventeen."

"What?"

"Just kidding," he said with a soft chuckle. "I have no idea, but you appear to have your breath back. It's time to move along."

Unsnapping her shackles and removing the cushion beneath her pelvis, he moved to the foot of the bed, unbuckling the leather straps, then suddenly grabbed her ankles and flipped her on her back.

She let out a squeal, then a happy laugh.

"Can we do that again? That was fun."

"I'll be doing that many times in the coming weeks," he promised. "Put your arms above your head."

Snapping her wrists back together and securing them to a rail in the headboard, he picked up the vibrator, powered it on, and thrust it inside her soaked passage. Holding it in place and leaning over her, he devoured her mouth in a crushing kiss. He knew it wouldn't be long before the stimulating dildo would rocket her into another orgasm, and as he pulled back and lowered his lip to suck in her breasts, he heard the telltale gasps and moans.

"I'm going to come again," she suddenly shouted. "I am. I can feel it."

"So soon?" he mumbled, raising his head, wondering if he should make her wait.

The thought came too late.

As she panted heavily and cried out her ecstasy, he moved the dildo in and out, milking her climax. Though fully aware the powerful vibrator could produce multiple orgasms, the suddenness of the onslaught had surprised him. When her spasms finally began to fade, he turned it off, placed it on the bed, and smoothed his hand across her body, waiting for her breathing to return to normal.

"You're somethin' else," he murmured, reaching up and removing her shackles. "I've gotta lot to learn about you, and I'm gonna love every lesson."

"Keith?" she murmured waving her arms in the air. "Keith, where are you?"

"Hey, babe, right here. The blindfold's stayin' on for a bit."

"I've never been through anything like that."

"Have you had enough?"

"Um, you said something about that-uh- dildo..." she muttered hesitantly.

"Are you up for it?"

"Probably not, but I want to try it."

"I absolutely adore you."

"Because I'm ready for more?"

"Because you're you," he replied, rolling her over.

Opening the drawer of his bedside table, he withdrew a small bottle of specially formulated massage oil. Pouring a dollop into his palms, he glided his hands down her back, briefly kneaded her backside, then slid his fingers inside her slick passage in search of her G-spot. Her gasp, then soft cry told him he'd found his target. Fingering her, and massaging the secret sensitive spot, he built her arousal until she begged him for his cock.

Kneeling between her legs and grabbing her hips, he pulled her into his pelvis. Sending his member inside her glorious channel, he rested his hands on her cheeks, pulled them apart, and gazed down at her virginal rosebud.

* * *

The lewd exposure sent a hot flush across her face, and she instinctively clenched.

"Let go of the fear and surrender Carly," he ordered sternly. "Ask me to keep going."

The command was what she'd needed.

"Please, Keith," she murmured, taking a deep breath. "Please keep going."

A dollop of something cool and tingly fell between her cheeks, then the vibrating dildo touched her dark hole and gently pushed forward.

Sparkling waves evoked a loud wail.

His cock began to thrust.

A powerful orgasm began to build.

A huge wall of water lifted her higher and higher...suddenly tumbling her through a whitewash of sizzling sensations.

* * *

Shrouded in the divine buzzing, with every stroke Keith had felt his climax loom. Plunging in and out of her hot, wet, scintillating channel, he'd tried to hold back, then her high-pitched cry catapulted him into his release.

Managing to keep his thumb pressed against the flange of the dildo, he erupted inside her. Convulsions rippled through his loins evoking loud, guttural groans, until the last spasm waned and his member slipped from her depths. Trying to catch his breath, he found her softly whimpering and lying limp beneath him.

Panting heavily, he switched off the dildo, carefully pulled it out and dropped it on the nightstand. Flopping next to her, his heart thumping wildly, he closed his eyes and willed it to settle.

* * *

Weightless, drained, and completely at peace, Carley barely felt the blindfold being removed, and blankets laid over her, but when Keith's arms came around her, she snuggled against him and fell into a serene sleep.

The following morning, she yawned, stretched, and yawned again, then rolled over to hug her cowboy. To her dismay he was gone, but her eye caught a folded note on the nightstand. Reaching across and opening it up, happy tears sprang to her eyes.

This cowboy loves you!

CHAPTER EIGHTEEN

Keith's long drive from the ranch to the airport was brightened when his phone rang and Carly's name appeared on the screen.

"Mornin' beautiful."

"This cowgirl loves you too," she said softly.

He caught his breath.

Leaving the heartfelt note had been spontaneous.

He'd had moments of doubt, wondering if he'd told her too soon, or should have waited to say it in person.

"What an amazing note to find," she continued. "This is the best morning of my life, except I wish you were here."

"There's nothin' I'd like better than to be curled up with you right now," he replied, a relieved smile curling his lips, "but I won't be gone long, and when I get back I'll have lots to tell you."

"I wouldn't care if you had nothing to tell me, just having you back will be enough for me. I don't like being in this bed without you, and, uh, last night," she murmured, her voice dropping, "Keith...there are no words..."

"Nope, I don't think there are," he muttered, thinking how his dominant soul had suffered through its long drought.

Then it hit him.

The bag in his closet.

He'd forgotten to hide it in his truck.

"Carly, I just remembered something. In the closet is a zippered sports bag. I need you to tuck it away in a corner of the closet out of sight."

"Okay. May I ask why?"

"Sure, in fact, you have permission to look inside. When you do you'll understand why I don't want Elsie stumbling across it."

"You mean, there's a bunch of wicked stuff in there?"

"Yep."

"Cool. I can't wait to take a peek, and don't worry, I'll make sure it's tucked away. Keith, I hate to say this, but I overslept and I need to get up."

"Overslept?" he repeated. "I can't imagine why."

"Neither can I," she quipped. "It's not like I was molested to within an inch of my life!"

"A whole inch? I'll have to fix that," he retorted with a chuckle. "You go shower and have your breakfast. I'll call you later," then lowering his voice he added, "Love you, babe."

"I love you too. You've made me so happy."

"Back at ya, beautiful."

Ending the call, his heart soared.

The woman of his dreams had walked through his door, and very soon he'd be living his life in the open. Being an oil company executive and building a successful ranch with his best friend and partner had been exhausting. If he lost his inheritance, so be it.

* * *

Happier than she ever remembered being, Carly showered and dressed, took a quick peek in the bag, then hurried down to the dining room. Andy had already come and gone, and Elsie was sitting at the table with a pad of paper and pen in her hand. Spying a tempting stack of pancakes, Carly sat down and eyed them hungrily.

"Good morning," Elsie said, smiling up at her. "Andy wanted flapjacks. Would you prefer something else?"

"No, thanks, these look great. I can't remember the last time I had a decadent breakfast like this."

"Help yourself. I have to run into town, but I won't be long. Don't worry about clearing things up. Do you need anything while I'm out?"

"No, but thanks for asking."

"Sorry to leave you to eat on your own," Elsie said, tearing the page from the pad and rising to her feet. "I always serve coffee and cake to our clients and I've run out of some things. I'll see you shortly."

As Elsie left, Carly lifted a pancake onto her plate, and was reaching for the maple syrup when her phone rang. Pulling it from her pocket she saw it was Andy. Hoping he wasn't calling to chase her up, she answered the call.

"Hi. I'm just finishing breakfast. Sorry if I'm late. I'll be right down."

"You don't have to be. Take your time. I wanna spend some time draggin' the ring."

"Do you want me to ride outside?"

"Did you forget? The horses get one day off a week, and that's today."

"Of course! There's been so much going on it slipped my mind. What about the horses we're showing?"

"They'll be stayin' in their paddocks. Connie Masters likes to watch them bein' brought in and tacked up. Most of the clients are like that."

"You mean I don't need to come down this morning?"

"Not unless you wanna ride Winston, otherwise you can take it easy."

"I'll pop down in a little bit and jump on my big boy. I know the buyers are coming at three, but what time do you want me there?"

"Two-forty-five would be good."

"Okay, Andy. Thanks. Bye."

"Bye."

Pushing her phone back in her pocket, Carly returned to her pancake. As she covered it with butter and syrup, her mind began to wander. She needed to call her parents. It would be easier to conference them so she didn't have to repeat her story, but she needed to talk to her father privately. She wanted to ask his help finding Salvo's sister, and speak to him about Gary, the man Elsie loved sitting in prison hoping to be paroled. Elsie was one of the kindest, warmest people Carly had ever met.

"Shoot. Dad will need Gary's last name," she muttered, pouring herself some coffee. "I'd better have a poke around before Elsie gets back."

Hastily finishing her breakfast, she hurried from the dining room and started down the hallway. Not sure where to start, Keith's office seemed the likeliest place. Though she was tempted to learn about Keith's father and Keith himself. Elsie's plight was foremost in her mind. Opening the door and walking in, she stood for a moment, staring around the room.

"What will I find in here about Elsie's boyfriend?" she muttered. "No, I need to go to her apartment, unless..."

Walking across to the bookshelf, she studied the photographs. There were many of Andy standing with well dressed people collecting trophies, various horses with gleaming coats in expensive frames with their names etched in brass plaques, but there were none of Keith or Elsie.

Then she spotted it.

At the very end of a shelf behind a bronze globe sat a photograph of two couples in elegant evening wear. Standing in front of them, she saw Keith as a young man. Intrigued, she stepped closer and carefully picked it up. She assumed they were his parents. The man was every bit as handsome as Keith, and the woman at his side was a stunning beauty. Next to them she recognized Elsie.

Dressed in a sparkling forest green gown, she smiled into the camera, but the man beside her stood a few feet away sporting a dour expression and his black hair and eyebrows gave him a sinister look.

"If you're Gary, you sure don't look very happy," she mumbled under her breath.

An idea unexpectedly popped into her head.

Turning it around, she carefully pushed back the thin, metal holders, then lifted away the velvet cover to reveal the back of the picture.

Her pulse ticking up, she tried to read the faded names. Finding it impossible, she moved to the window to view the writing in better light.

"Mable and Elsie," she muttered, "but what does that say? Harry? No, it's Harlan. His father's name is Harlan. Where's Keith? That's weird, I think that says Heath? Who the hell is Heath? Does Keith have a twin brother?"

"Heath is Keith's second cousin."

Spinning around, turning beet red, she saw Elsie standing in the doorway.

"The man next to me is my ex-husband, Brice. He was extremely nasty. Please put the photo back."

"Elsie, this isn't what it looks like, I swear."

"What else could it be?" she asked with a heavy frown. "You're in Keith's office studying a personal picture. Obviously you're trying to delve into his past. Carly, I'm surprised at you."

"Please let me explain," Carly said hastily, placing the photograph back in its frame. "Honestly, I have a very good reason for doing this. Two very good reasons, but I can only tell you about one of them."

"Excuse me?"

"Good grief. Okay, I have to confess something you're not going to like."

"I'm already seeing something I don't like."

"I know, but it will make sense in a minute," Carly promised, returning the picture to the shelf, then perching on the arm of the nearby couch. "I overheard your conversation with Keith about your friend Gary. I was looking for information about him so I could help, but without his last name that's impossible."

"You eavesdropped?"

"Not exactly, well, kind of. I knew Keith was going to tell you about us, and I just wanted to hear what he said about me. I wasn't motivated by nosiness, I was motivated by my heart. I'm crazy about him, but that's beside the point. Elsie, the thing is, I can help your friend Gary, or rather, my father can."

"What kind of help?" Elsie asked warily, moving closer.

"I heard you say you're worried Keith's dad might interfere with the parole board."

"Gary's in prison for cocaine possession. He might be a nefarious drug dealer for all you know. Why would you want to become involved?"

"The man who refused to even take an aspirin is a nefarious drug dealer?" Carly replied, raising her eyebrows. "I doubt it. Elsie, I was going to help without you knowing, but you've caught me. All I needed was Gary's last name. Am I curious about Keith? Of course, but my sole purpose this morning was finding information about Gary so I could pass it along to my father."

"But again I must ask you, why? We're virtual strangers."

"You've welcomed me here and treated me with nothing but warmth and kindness. And as I just said, I'm crazy about Keith. Of course I want to help."

"My goodness," Elsie said, staring at her. "I'm at a loss for words."

"Do you think Keith's father will try to interfere with Gary's parole?"

"He might," Elsie replied, her frown deepening. "I don't have anything to do with him anymore, but from what Keith has told me, he's become extremely unpredictable. He's changed so much. My brother and I were once very close."

"I'm sorry, Elsie. Please will you let me help you?"

"But how can you?"

"Is Gary in Bellworth?"

"He is. Why?"

"Can we take this conversation back to the table and talk over a cup of coffee?" Carly suggested. "There's a lot I need to tell you. When I'm done you'll understand."

* * *

While Carly and Elsie were deep in conversation in Keith's office, inside the garage, the sandy-haired man had climbed from the trunk of Elsie's car.

A short time before, he'd been sitting outside the local cafe drinking coffee. He'd been so shocked to see a woman who looked exactly like Elsie, he'd spilled his drink. She'd been climbing from a silver Buick sedan, and as she'd walked through the neighboring parking lot, he'd leaned forward and scrutinized her. His lip curled in a snarl.

"Found you, bitch," he'd grunted, and throwing money on the table, he'd hurried across the small lane and made a beeline for her car. There was no-one around. The feature of small towns he'd always hated, now worked to his advantage. Shooting a last quick glance around the lot, he'd tried the driver's door. Finding it unlocked, he'd leaned in, found the button, and popped the trunk. Hurrying around the car, he found the space large and empty, with an emergency escape pull.

The opportunity had been too good to pass up.

Making sure no-one was watching from a vantage point he'd missed, he'd quickly climbed in and pulled it closed.

The drive had been amazingly smooth.

Now emerging, he found himself in a dark garage.

Retrieving his phone and turning on the flashlight, he spotted a door he assumed led into the house. Quietly closing the trunk, he crept forward. Hearing nothing, he turned off his phone, pushed the door open, and peered into the large empty kitchen.

Creeping inside, he moved across to a swinging door, paused, cracked it open and peered inside. On the table sat a stack of pancakes, and a dish laden with syrup. Wondering if breakfast had been interrupted, he moved quickly into the room, grabbed two of the pancakes, gobbled them down, then walked to the open doorway and stared down the empty hall.

"Fuck this place is big," he muttered, moving slowly forward.

Suddenly hearing voices, he ducked into the first door.

They were female, and watching through the door jamb he saw Elsie and the pretty young woman he'd seen on the grounds walking towards the dining room. Assuming the two men would be working, he broke into an evil smile. It had taken a lot of time and effort, but he'd finally struck gold.

He'd take his time, do some exploring, then make his move.

CHAPTER NINETEEN

The flight to Houston had been uneventful. Keith used the time thinking through what he would say to his father and how he would say it. A company car was waiting, and climbing into the back seat, he pulled out his phone and called Carly. He wanted and needed to hear her voice. He would soon be in a conversation he dreaded, yet couldn't wait to have.

"Keith! How great to hear from you," she exclaimed. "Was your flight okay?"

"Yes, fine. How are you?"

"Great, except I miss you. Andy wanted to work on the footing in the ring and I'd planned to ride Winston, but Elsie and I have been hanging out."

"I'm glad. You two should get to know each other better."

"That's what we're doing."

"Okay, babe, I'll call you again soon."

"Please do. Hearing your voice is wonderful."

"Yours too."

The car was already out of the airport, and as he leaned back and stared out the window, he thought about how much his father had changed.

When his mother had passed away, Harlan Boyd had been mad at the world, but Keith still didn't believe he would have framed Gary Campbell, especially using drugs to do it. That just wasn't his style. He would have hired lawyers to covertly dig into Gary's business for evidence of wrongdoing, then turned it over to the authorities.

Though Keith had been in the house when Elsie had tearfully accused Harlan of the hateful act, Keith had never discussed it with him. Now he was determined to learn the truth, whatever that was, and lay it to rest once and for all.

As his phone chimed and broke into his thoughts, he wasn't surprised to see it was the man himself.

"Hey, dad, I was just about to call you. We're exiting the freeway now. I'll be in River Oaks shortly."

"Good flight?"

"Is there such a thing anymore?"

"If you stayed here in Houston like you should, you could use the company jet whenever you wanted."

"I'll keep that in mind."

"Mitzi is at the house and she'll be joining us for dinner, but I'll meet you at the restaurant. I'm still in the office."

"Has anyone ever mentioned you work too hard?"

"When you love what you do, there's no work involved," Harlan retorted. "That's something you need to learn."

"I have already, dad, a while back."

"Does that mean you're loving your job now? Has your old man's company finally won you over?"

"Not exactly, but dad, I don't want to go out to dinner. Can you just come home?"

"Sure, if you want. Did I tell you I've hired a chef? He's pretty damn good."

"No, but I'm sure he is."

"I'll see you later, son."

"Okay. Bye, dad."

With a heavy sigh Keith ended the call. He was entering the exclusive neighborhood, and though he admired the magnificent homes, none were as appealing as his rambling log cabin on the knoll. Turning into the sweeping driveway, the car rolled to a stop, and as he stepped out, Mitzi opened the front door and walked quickly forward to greet him.

"I'm so relieved you're here," she said earnestly, hurrying forward to meet him. "I need to talk to you."

"Hi Mitzi, what's wrong?"

"Your father," she declared as they entered the two-story foyer with its polished marble floors. "I'm worried sick."

"Why?"

"I'm sorry, sugar. Do you need to go up to your room and freshen up?"

"No, I'm fine," he said, dropping his bag. "Let's go into the front room and you can tell me what's goin' on."

"Thank you, thank you," she gushed, leading him into the comfortable living room. "Sit next to me. I need to keep my voice down. Servants gossip."

"You have more than just the housekeeper?"

"Harlan doesn't want me cooking. He hired a chef, and even though we have a full-time housekeeper, someone comes in and does the floors three days a week."

"Honestly, I'm not surprised. Mom had both."

"But your mother entertained, and she had you to run around after."

"This is true."

"I'd like to downsize," Mitzi mumbled, "but anyway, about your father."

"Yes, about my father. What's got you so wound up?"

"He's working night and day."

"He's always worked night and day."

"Not like this," she said emphatically. "He's out of bed at the crack of dawn, and he stays up all night. He used to come to bed around eleven and we'd watch the news together, but now he's in his office downstairs on the phone, or pacing around the house. Then he'll suddenly crash. You'll see. His eyes are puffy with dark circles around them, they're always red, and he's been losing weight. I don't know what's wrong with him."

"Huh. That sounds extreme even for him," Keith said thoughtfully. "I was here six weeks ago and I remember some of that, but I only saw him briefly."

"I'm telling you, Heath, things aren't right, and they're getting worse. Please will you talk to him? You know he adores you."

"Uh, sure, of course I'll talk to him, but I'm not sure he'll listen."

"Thank you, sugar."

"I'm glad you told me, but I can't promise anything. Speaking of being up at the crack of dawn, if you'll excuse me I'm going up to my room for a shower and a nap."

"Is there anything special you'd like for dinner? Anton cooks everything."

"Anton? That's the name of your chef? Is he French or Italian?"

"I have no idea."

"I don't care," Keith said with a grin. "Surprise me."

"I can't tell you how relieved I am you're here. I've been praying you'd show up. I sure hope you can get some answers."

"I'll do my best."

* * *

Back at Dream Horse Ranch, sitting at the dining room table with a pad and pen, Carly had written down everything Elsie had just told her, but picking up the phone to call her father she paused.

"Is something the matter?" Elsie asked.

"No, not at all. I have to tell both mom and dad about the accident. I'd like to conference them in, then keep dad on the line..."

"Why am I hearing a but at the end of that sentence?"

"It'll be a war, it always is."

"If you don't mind me asking, is this why you wanted to live in a small town on a quiet ranch?"

"That's exactly why," Carly replied with a sigh, "and I was tired of the craziness of the show barns. Now that I think about it, I don't want to listen to them squabble. I'll call my dad, then I'll call mom. Hopefully he won't be playing golf," she said as she placed the call.

"Sweetheart, what a lovely surprise," her father said, answering immediately.

"Hi dad."

"How's the new job?"

"Fantastic."

"Are you calling to say hello or is there something going on?"

"Uh, do you want to hear the bad news first, or the favor?"

"The bad news."

"Daisy got smashed by an airborne tree branch in a windstorm. She's completely wrecked."

"What? Are you okay?"

"Yes, I'm fine, but what should I do about the insurance?"

"Send me the pictures and I'll contact the agent. Think about what you'd like to replace it with, and please, Carly, I'm begging you, let me buy you a nice new modern vehicle that has airbags and four-wheel disc brakes, maybe even four-wheel drive. I know you like your independence, but your poor old dad was worried sick with you driving around in that—"

"Careful, dad."

"I was going to say, that beautifully renovated classic. It was pretty, but it wasn't safe!"

"That's really sweet of you dad, but—"

"Don't say but. Please just think about it."

"Okay, I'll think about it."

"What's the favor?"

"Uh, there's more than one."

"You can ask as many as you want. I'll grant them all if you let me buy you something *new*."

"You never give up."

"Not where you're welfare is concerned. What are the favors?"

"There's a lovely lady who works here and I'm pretty sure her boyfriend was railroaded. He's in Bellworth and he's up for parole in a couple of weeks. Can you look at the file? See if there's anything there that screams foul? The second is, she's worried that someone might try to interfere with his hearing. Is there anything you can do about that?"

"Put her on the phone, please."

"Sure. Her name is Elsie. Here you go, Elsie," Carly said, handing her the phone. "Dad needs to talk to you."

"Mr. Kincaid, I'm sorry if this is an imposition."

"Please, call me Michael, and this is no imposition. What's your friend's name and who was his attorney?"

"Gary Campbell is my friend, and his attorney was Jim Bolson."

"Uh-huh. How did your friend end up with Jim Bolson?"

"I don't know. I never asked."

"Do you have a fax there?"

"Yes."

"I'm going to send you over an agreement. It will state that you're retaining my services for one-dollar. Sign it and fax it back to me, then I can have Bolson turn over your friend's file."

"This is so kind of you, thank you."

"You're very welcome and Elsie, I'm fairly confident I'll find something."

"Really?" she asked, her heart skipping. "You think so?"

"I do. Jim Bolson isn't the sharpest of lawyers. Who do you think will try to interfere in the parole process. That's serious."

"Uh, Harlan Boyd."

Carly's jaw dropped.

Keith's father was a famous oil tycoon.

"Excuse me, Elsie," Michael said slowly, "just so I understand, are you talking about Harlan Boyd of Boyd Holdings?"

"Yes, he's my brother. Mr. Kincaid—sorry—Michael, may I ask you something?"

"Of course. I'm your lawyer, or soon will be. You can ask me anything."

"Carly told me you're a criminal defense attorney, but she didn't say how you could help with the parole hearing."

"I'm also a parole lawyer, and let me assure you, it is highly unlikely that anyone, not even Harlan Boyd, would be able to influence your friend's parole. I'll look over his case, and I'm happy to represent him at the hearing. When is it?"

"In two weeks."

"That doesn't give me much time. Get that paperwork back to me as soon as you can. What's your fax number?"

Though Carly had been staring at the stack of pancakes, her mind had suddenly switched gears when she'd heard the shocking news that Harlan Boyd was Keith's father.

"Your dad wants to say goodbye."

"Oh, of course," she said, snapping up her head. "Hey, dad."

"That's quite a connection you've made. Harlan Boyd's sister?"

"It was news to me, and there's more but it will have to wait."

"You've been a busy girl."

"I plead the fifth. Can I ask about the next favor?"

"Can I buy you a new car?"

"Dad!"

"That question requires a yes or no answer."

"I said I'll think about it and I will. That P.I. Does he still work for you?"

"Mitch? Yes, he does."

"I need him to find someone for me. Is that okay?"

"Sure, but can you tell me who and why?"

"I'll text you the information right now."

"What do you want him to do if he finds this person?"

"Just send me the information. I have a feeling this will be easy."

"Anything else?"

"No, daddy, except thank you, and I love you to bits."

"You're welcome, sweetheart. Come and visit me soon."

"I will, I promise."

Ending the call, she immediately texted him Theresa's name and the smattering of history she had, then dropped the phone on the table.

"Harlan Boyd?" she said, staring at Elsie wide-eyed. "I assume Keith Parker is Heath Boyd. Holy crap. I thought he looked familiar when I met him. Why is he hiding out under a different name? Can you tell me anything at all?"

"I suppose there's no reason why I shouldn't at this point," Elsie replied with a resigned sigh. "Andy and I liked the name Keith because it sounded like Heath and made it less likely we'd slip up. All Heath ever wanted was to be a cowboy. A few years back, he and Andy decided to team up. Andy didn't have the money or business experience, and Heath didn't have Andy's horsemanship skills."

"But why the secrecy?"

"I'm getting to that. Harlan has always been hell-bent on Heath taking over Boyd Holdings. Heath was raised inside that company, but every chance he got, he was at the barn where his mother rode. He just loved being with the horses. When he graduated, he wanted to break free from his dad and start up his own ranch. The only way he could do it was on the sly, but it had to be far away from Houston. He's too well-known, and if his father found out—there'd be hell to pay. So for several years, Heath has been living a double life."

"Good grief."

"About the same time Heath found this place and decided to take the leap of faith, Gary was arrested, and I fell out with Harlan. It was a bad time, but Heath asked if I would join him and help with the house. Coming was a lifeline."

"This is unbelievable," Carly murmured, shaking her head.

"If someone recognized him here, and decided to make a quick buck and contact the tabloids, all hell would break loose. Heath is still dependent on his income from Boyd Holdings to keep the ranch running."

"I'm in shock. Honestly, I am."

"I probably should have let him tell you all that, and he was planning on it, but there you have it. Everything has come to a head. He's gone to Houston to tell his father everything, and Carly, I believe you're a big part of the reason why."

"Me?"

"He's not a naturally duplicitous person, and being so secretive with you wasn't sitting well with him. He'd started hitting the wall a few months back, and I think you're the straw that broke the camel's back."

"Starving cowboy or a rich one, I don't care," Carly exclaimed. "The moment when I first came here, my stomach was in knots. Now I'm so in love with that man I can hardly stand it. In fact, I was sitting here missing him like mad, and apparently I ate two more pancakes than I thought. How's that for crazy?"

Tilting her head to the side Elsie stared at the stack.

"There are three left..." she murmured, a frown crossing her brow. "But when I came in from the store, I checked, and I wondered why you'd only eaten one. I made half-a-dozen. There should be five."

"If that's true then...huh...maybe Salvo or Andy have been up here."

"It wasn't Andy. He was on that tractor dragging the arena when I left, and still there when I got back. Salvo would never let himself in, never. He always calls first, and knocks on the door unless he's been invited."

"But it has to be one of them. Who else would come in here and take two pancakes?"

"That would be me," the sandy-haired man declared walking in from the hallway. "Hello, Elsie love. Aren't you happy to see me? Our anniversary is in two days, or had you forgotten?"

CHAPTER TWENTY

Carly immediately recognized the tall scraggly man in the doorway as the worker she'd seen the day before.

"I don't know what you want," Carly exclaimed, jumping to her feet and scowling at him, "but you'd better get the hell out of here."

"Sure, I'll be happy to leave, but not without my wife."

Though taken off guard, as she hastily studied his face, she realized he was the dour man in the photograph next to Elsie. He'd bleached his hair and his eyebrows were thinner, but it was him.

"Brice, I am not your wife!" Elsie exclaimed. "What's wrong with you? Have you completely lost your mind?"

"I told you if you left me I'd ruin your brother, and if you went out with anyone else I'd ruin him too."

"But—but—that was years ago."

"I'm a patient man, Elsie, and I've done both. I knew you'd be hiding out with your snot-nosed nephew. I just had a helluva time finding him, but now he's going down too. Before we leave I'm going to burn this place to the ground."

"It was you?" she gasped, her eyes wide. "All this time I've been blaming Harlan, and you were the one who planted that cash and cocaine in Gary's house?"

"Yep," the man said proudly, puffing out his chest, "but I decided a simple arrest was too good for your brother. That snake threatened me one too many times."

"What have you done to him?"

"Hah. Wouldn't you like to know? I'm going to let you stew on that for a while. Maybe I'll tell you when we go out to dinner for our anniversary."

"I'm not going anywhere with you!" she yelled. "Not ever."

"Yeah, you will, but I'm gonna have some fun with your little friend here. There's a real fancy bedroom at the end of the hall," he sneered, pulling a pistol from a shoulder holster. "What's your name gorgeous?"

"Go fuck yourself," Carly retorted, feigning a confidence she didn't feel.

"Huh, that's an unusual name. I think I'll call you Kitty. Time to stretch out on the bed, Kitty."

"Don't you dare touch her," Elsie said vehemently. "I'll go with you, but only if you leave her alone."

"You stupid bitch. That deal's off the table now, but don't worry, you'll be coming with me when I leave. I just want some fun before we take off, although, maybe I'll take her along and she can work for us. Yeah, I'd sure like to see her in a sexy maid's outfit."

"Excuse me," Carly said angrily, "if anyone's stupid around here, that's you. The guys here will be walking in that door any minute to finish their breakfast."

"Nice try. You've only got two hicks here. One is dragging the ring, and that Salvo kid is putting up a new carport, but if they do show up, I'm more than happy to put a bullet between their eyes."

Carly searched frantically for a way to stall.

Her phone suddenly rang.

Her eyes darted to the screen.

The caller was her mother.

It was a miracle.

"This is my mom," she declared. "If I don't answer she'll know something's wrong. She calls me every day at this time to make sure I'm all right."

Brice eyed her suspiciously.

"I'm serious. I had an accident in my truck during that windstorm and she's calling to see if I'm okay. If I don't pick up, she'll ask Salvo or Andy to check the house."

"Fuck. Put it on speaker, and if you say anything you shouldn't I'll pulverize Elsie's face."

"Sure, no problem," Carly said hastily, her heart racing as she answered the call. "Hi, Mom."

"Hello, honey. What's this about you getting hurt in that old truck? Tell me. I want to hear every last detail."

"It was nothing serious. I just hurt my shoulder, but it's fine. Uh, mom, I can't talk at the moment, though there is something you should know."

"What's more important than your truck getting crunched by a tree with you inside?"

"It was just a branch, but mom, I'm having lunch with Roger tomorrow."

There was a pause.

"Mom, did you hear me? I know this is a surprise, but yes, I'm having lunch with Roger tomorrow. He came here unexpectedly."

"Roger? Are you serious?"

"Yes, very."

"Where?"

"Here at the ranch. We'll be dining in the main house."

"I'll let your father know right away."

"Thanks, that saves me a call. I need to get off the phone now, but I love you mom, and when you talk to dad tell him I love him too."

"I love you too, honey. Call me back when you can talk about the accident."

"Sure will."

"Bye."

"Bye."

"Leave your fucking phone where it is and let's go," Brice said sharply, waving the gun towards the hall. "Straight to that fancy bedroom. Do anything stupid and trust me, you'll be sorry."

* * *

In the wood-paneled den in Harlan's luxurious home in Houston, Heath had just confessed the truth. He had been executing his work at Boyd Holdings while building a horse training and sales barn. To his surprise, his father had listened intently, then wordlessly nodded his head.

"So you see, dad, I haven't been travelin' like you think. I've been workin' from my office at the ranch," Heath continued. "I know this is a huge disappointment, and I'm sorry about that, but horses are in my blood. I can't sit in one of those glass cages and stare out at buildings all day. So, uh, I'm here to hand in my resignation."

"You're just like your mother," Harlan mumbled. "You get this horse thing from her."

"You used to say that when I'd leave to go to the barn with her. You weren't wrong then, and you're not wrong now, but it's not something I'm ashamed of. I'm good at what I do, real good, and I—"

"I should've bought a ranch for the two of you back then," Harlan muttered, cutting him off, "but I thought you'd fall off one of those damn broncs and kill yourself."

"Dad, are you all right? You're takin' this really well. I thought you'd go ballistic."

"I'm real tired today, son," Harlan replied wearily.

"You weren't tired when I spoke to you from the car. You sounded great."

"I have energy, then it goes away."

"So, you're okay with this? My ranch, I mean."

"Hell, no I'm not okay with it!" Harlan suddenly barked. "I want you to take over the business, but I've known for a long time your heart's not in it."

"You have?"

"It was obvious. I'm not an idiot. You would have been with me night and day, so yeah, I'm okay with you and your ranch," he finished, his voice abruptly softening and letting out a heavy sigh.

"Uh, dad, you said you're not okay with it," Heath said slowly, "but just now you said you are. Which is it?"

"Ssh. I'm listening to your mother."

"Dad, what are you—?"

"Hush, your mother's talking to me," Harlan snapped. "She's saying you need to blaze your own trail. Yep, I agree, Mabel. Ticks me off, but what matters most is that he's happy."

"Something's wrong with you," Heath mumbled, watching his father roll his eyes back and stare at the ceiling. "Dad, I need to talk to Mitzi. I'll be back in a minute."

"Mitzi? Lovely girl. Lovely. Yeah, you find Mitzi. Make sure she tells Anton I want something creamy for dinner. No. Something fishy. The hell with it. Something that tastes good, that's it, something that tastes good."

Deeply concerned, Heath rose to his feet to leave, but Mitzi suddenly burst into the room looking as anxious as he felt.

"Heath, you have a phone call from someone named Michael Kincaid. He says he needs to speak to you urgently."

"Kincaid?" he repeated, quickly realizing the caller had to be Carly's father.

"You can take it over there," she said, pointing to a phone on Harlan's desk.

"Thanks. Listen, Mitzi, you need to get Doctor Hendricks over here right away. Something's wrong with dad."

"See? I told you. I'll call him right away."

As she hurriedly left the room, Heath strode across to the desk and picked up the house phone.

"This is Heath Boyd."

"Hello, Heath. I'm Carly's father. I'm sorry for this urgent call, but she's in trouble. Can you send someone to check the house?"

"Of course, but what kind of trouble?"

"I don't know," Michael said hastily. "When Carly was dating, her mother insisted on a safety code. If Carly called and said, I'm having lunch with Roger tomorrow, it meant, I'm in a life-threatening situation. Erin was supposed to ask where she was, and Carly would give her a clue. Of course nothing ever happened, but now it has. Her mother just called and that's what Carly said. She's in the house and something is horribly wrong."

"Oh, my God! I see your number. I'll call you right back."

Without waiting for a reply, Heath hung up the receiver, snatched his cellphone from his pocket, and called Andy, but it was answered by voicemail.

"Dammit, Andy, Carly's in trouble up in the house," Heath exclaimed. "I don't know what kind of trouble so be careful, but get up there now. I'm calling Salvo."

Fighting a rising panic as he tried to stay calm, he placed the call.

"Hi, Keith. What's—"

"Salvo, Carly's in trouble."

"Where? What's happened?"

"In the house. There must be an intruder or something. All I know is she's in danger. I tried to reach Andy but his phone went to voicemail."

"He's still working on the tractor. He probably didn't hear his phone."

"Call the police, then get Andy and go up there, but be careful. Don't go bursting inside. Try to find out what's going on. Let me know the minute you find out."

"On my way."

As Heath ended the call, Mitzi appeared and raced over to him.

"Heath, I reached Doctor Hendricks. He'll be here in about thirty minutes."

"That's great. Talk to dad while we're waitin'. See if you can find out if he's taken anything. If I didn't know better, I'd say he's on drugs."

"I found some pills in one of his pockets about a month ago."

"Pills? What kind of pills?"

"I don't know. They were in a small plastic bag. He said they made him think clearly and gave him energy."

"Dammit. Go and stay with him," Heath said, picking up the house phone and calling Carly's father. "I'll be right there."

Michael Kincaid answered on the first ring.

"Heath? What's going on?"

"My guys are callin' the police and goin' up to the house, but I find it hard to believe there's an intruder. There's no way to get on the property without goin' through the front gates, and you can't climb over them."

"She wouldn't have used that code without cause."

"Of course she wouldn't. I'll stay in touch. I'm sure I'll hear something soon."

"Thanks, Heath. I'll be waiting."

Placing the receiver back on the cradle, and wishing he hadn't left the ranch, Heath lowered his eyes and touched his key.

"Mom, if you are watching over us, please help Carly."

Slowly lifting his gaze to the family pictures hanging on the wall behind his father's desk, he found himself drawn to an old photograph of Elsie and her former husband.

He caught his breath.

"Brice! It was you at the ranch yesterday. You've bleached your hair, but that was you! Why? What the hell is goin' on?"

CHAPTER TWENTY-ONE

Anxiously walking down the long hall towards the bedroom, Carly believed Brice was capable of doing exactly what he threatened. Elsie was panic stricken, and though help would arrive, Carly didn't see waiting as an option. Entering the bedroom, she searched desperately for a weapon. When her eyes fell on the closet door, she remembered glimpsing something when she'd pushed the sports bag into a corner behind the hanging clothes.

Her heart began to race.

Her plan was risky at best.

She had to try.

They were almost at the bed.

She needed another miracle...

A tremendous crash suddenly echoed through the room.

The large photograph of the barn and paddocks had fallen off its hook spraying fragments of glass across the room.

Elsie screamed.

Brice spun around.

Carly sprinted into the closet and hastily closed the door.

Racing to the far corner and jerking away the bag, she hastily snatched up the bolt-action rifle and checked the chamber.

It was loaded.

Rushing to the front of the closet, she stood with her back against the wall.

Every part of her body trembled.

The door slowly opened.

Stepping inside, Brice held the gun out in front of him, his arm extended.

"Here, kitty, kitty, kitty. Come on, kitty, time to say you're sorry."

Swiftly raising the rifle, Carly smashed the steel barrel down on his hand. As he howled in shock and pain, the pistol fell from his fingers.

"Back up," she barked, aiming the rifle directly at his head as he staggered sideways. "I know how to use this. Now back the fuck up."

"Stupid cow," he snarled, moving towards her. "Go ahead, shoot me. Go ahead. You don't have the guts."

"You don't know me asshole."

He hesitated.

It was all she needed.

Fiercely kicking up her foot, it landed against his crotch. Yowling loudly and grabbing himself, he fell on the floor and doubled over.

Swiftly booting his pistol out the door, she raced back to the bag of wicked toys and hastily pulled out the handcuffs. But turning around, she realized getting them on his wrists would be impossible.

His scrawny legs were visible below his jeans, and curled up in a fetal position his feet were together. Laying down the rifle and holding her breath, she crawled forward on her hands and knees, and swiftly snapped the cuffs around his ankles.

"Fuck you!" he wailed, abruptly jerking his legs and sitting up.

"Shut up and keep still," she shouted, snatching up the rifle, "or I swear to God I'll castrate you, and believe me, that I can do."

"Try it bitch, try it!"

She needed to get past him and out the door, but with his long arms it was too risky. Glancing around for an idea, she spied a bedspread on a shelf above her head. Leaning the rifle against the back wall, she pulled the coverlet down and flapped it over him.

"Bitch!" he screamed, writhing beneath the king-sized cover.

Grabbing the rifle and scooting past him, she dashed out the door and slammed it shut, only to find Elsie lying on the bed with her hands tied behind her with a belt.

"Carly, thank God," she whimpered. "What happened in there? Are you okay?"

"I'm fine, and he's not going anywhere," Carly said confidently, sliding the rifle under the bed and picking up tissues from the nightstand. "What about you?"

"All right," she replied breathlessly, "but what are you doing?"

"Fingerprints. My dad's a criminal defense lawyer, remember? I don't want to contaminate the evidence."

Carefully untying the belt, she laid it out, then helped Elsie off the bed.

"Come on Elsie, sit on the chair by the fireplace," she said softly, putting her arm around the quivering woman.

"What about B-Brice? Are you sure he c-can't get out of there?"

"His ankles are cuffed. Shit. I have no idea where the key is. I guess he'll stay that way for a while."

"How did you manage that?" Elsie asked, staring at her as she settled into the comfortable arm chair.

"It doesn't matter. You just catch your breath. I'll get us some help."

Hurrying to the bedside table and picking up the phone, she hastily called Andy.

"Hello?" Andy said anxiously.

"Andy, it's Carly. Where are you?"

"Half-way down the hall. Where are you? Are you okay?"

"Thank God. Yes, I'm fine, I'm in Keith's, sorry, Heath's bedroom with Elsie. Get in here, and hurry."

* * *

When the physician arrived at the Boyd home, it took him only a couple of minutes with Harlan before suggesting drug use, then he'd asked Heath to leave.

Pacing around the den as this father's examination continued, Heath was beside himself with worry for his father, and desperate for news from the ranch. When his cell phone rang and he saw Carly's name on the screen, his heart leapt.

"Tell me you're not hurt," he said anxiously as he answered the call. "Tell me Elsie's okay."

"We're both fine, and I'm so happy to hear your voice. I wish you were here. I need you."

"I wish I was there too. Was there an intruder? What about Andy? Who's there with you?"

"Andy and Salvo are both here and the Sheriff has just arrived. I'll tell you all the details later, but yeah, we had an intruder. It was Elsie's ex-husband. Apparently he's been hunting Elsie for ages."

"I can't believe what I'm hearin'. So many years have passed."

"I know, and I also know you're Heath Boyd and why you had to be so secretive."

"You do?" he muttered, his pulse ticking up.

"Heath, I completely understand."

"I'm sorry I couldn't tell you."

"Honestly, I get it. There's no problem, but I have to tell you something else. It was Brice who set up Gary Campbell, and he said he was ruining your father's life too, but he didn't say how. Is your dad okay?"

"Damn. I know exactly what he meant," Heath said grimly. "Our doctor is here. Dad's on a drug of some kind. Brice must have managed to get him hooked. That's why he's been so crazy."

"No!"

"He'll be goin' into a private facility for a while."

"I'm so sorry."

"Hey, he's alive, but he was really out of it when I got here. He was talkin' gibberish."

"When are you coming home?"

"It'll be a few days. I need to get him checked in and meet with some people at the company."

"Is there anything I can do to help?"

"Hey, why don't you come and join me. You could visit your dad."

"That's a great idea. Yes, I'd love to. And Elsie as well. I think she could use a few days away."

"Definitely, but what about showin' the horses today? The buyers are supposed to be there..when? In an hour? Two hours? I've completely lost track of time."

"We still have a couple of hours before they get here, and I've already told Andy I'm absolutely fine. The sheriff and his deputies will be long gone."

"Are you sure you're up to it?"

"Absolutely. I'm just sorry you won't be here."

"But I'll be watchin'."

"How?"

"We have cameras, remember? Make sure you text me when the clients arrive. All I have to do is open up my laptop."

"That's fantastic. I totally forgot."

"And you're sure you're okay?"

"My pulse is still racing a bit, but I'm going down to the barn. There's nothing that calms me more than being with Winston, except maybe—you know," she said softly.

"Damn I miss you. I'm going to send the company jet."

"Me? On a private jet? You're kidding?"

"That's the fastest way I know to get you here. I'm dyin' to know what happened, and I've got a very strong feelin' it was you who saved the day."

"You can thank my mother—and yours."

"What?"

"I'll explain later. I need to go. A detective just walked in and wants to talk to me."

"Carly, I love you," he said softly, fighting the wave of emotion threatening to sweep him away. "I've been so damn worried."

"I love you too, Heath, more than I can say."

"It feels good to hear you say my real name."

"Yeah? I'm glad, but that was a bit weird for me. Not to worry. I'll get used to it, and it suits you better."

"It does?"

"Totally. Now I really do need to go. The detective is frowning."

"I'll call you with the flight details soon."

"Fantastic. I can't wait to be with you."

"Me too, babe, me too."

* * *

Three hours later, two black Cadillac SUV's rolled through the gates of Dream Horse Ranch, and Andy stepped up to meet them as they rolled to a stop in front of the barn. As the well-heeled visitors stepped from their vehicles, pleasantries were exchanged, then Connie Masters, along with three trainers and several other buyers, walked across to the paddocks to study the horses.

Already waiting at the gate, Carly entered Domino's pasture, and the moment she entered his paddock, the horse ambled across to her and dropped its head into her chest. Lifting her eyes, Carly recognized the envy in Connie Master's face. It was obvious she wanted that kind of connection to a horse. Carly wasn't surprised. She'd often witnessed the frustration of others who didn't understand what it took to develop a kinship with their equine.

"Have you been handling this horse very long?" Connie asked as they walked up to the barn. "You seem very attached."

"I've only been here a short time. I actually rode him for the first time yesterday."

"How is that possible?" Connie asked, standing back while Carly led him into the cross ties. "How can you get close to a horse so quickly?"

"Horses are all about energy," Carly replied, scratching his ears. "They pick up what you're feeling. Confidence and love, that's what I give them. If they have an issue when I'm riding, they're either confused, afraid, or in pain. I do my best to find out which it is. Most of the time it's confusion."

"Confusion about what?"

"What I want. Especially in the beginning. There are basic aids, sure, but some riders are soft, some strong, some kick, some squeeze. Most humans expect the poor horse to know. But sometimes there's a physical problem. Horses don't get anxious for no reason."

"She's right," Andy declared. "She figured out Preston had somethin' goin' on with his mouth. She rode him in a halter and he was fine."

"Preston? The big black beauty?"

"Yep."

"Can I see her ride him like that?"

"Sure, but nothin' fancy," Andy replied. "We don't know how much his mouth is botherin' him."

"Thanks. Let's go up to the viewing area," Connie said, still watching Carly groom Domino. "I'm dying to see this horse under saddle."

As Connie walked away, Carly saw two of the trainers and a couple of other people she assumed were buyers, take Andy aside and speak with him before following Connie up the stairs. Walking back to the cross-ties to help her finish tacking up, he grinned and lowered his head.

"No pressure, but if you do good there's gonna be a biddin' war."

"For Domino?"

"No, Carly, for you. They want to know how much you charge."

"To do what?"

"Train, ride, whatever."

"Seriously? Huh. Well, I'm flattered, but I'm not interested. This is my home now."

"I was hopin' you'd say that," Andy said with a grin. "I had to tell you though. What you do with that God-given talent of yours is up to you."

"I don't know how talented I am, but I do know how much I love these amazing animals."

As if understanding her, Domino gave her a nudge.

"I swear, you talk horse, girl. I'm goin' up to join them. I'd wish you luck but I know you don't need it."

"I'll take it anyway," she said with a grin. "Any last suggestions?"

"Smile. It looks good on you."

* * *

Propped up on his bed with his laptop open, Heath had followed the goings on at the barn. When Carly had said, *this is my home now,* he'd wanted to climb through the screen and hug her. Now watching her put Domino through his paces his heart swelled with pride. The horse was sheer perfection. As she climbed off and led him from the ring, Heath waited five minutes then called her.

"Hi, did you see it?" she asked breathlessly.

"Carly, there are no words. You were brilliant. I'm so proud of you."

"I was a passenger. Domino is a dream."

"No, you never just ride. You silently talk to a horse unlike anyone I've ever seen, and how you were able to do that after everything that happened with Brice is absolutely amazin'. You're amazin'."

He waited for her to respond, but all he could hear was her breathing.

"Carly?"

"I'm sorry. Just give me a minute."

"What is it? Did I upset you?"

"I didn't know I could feel like this," she murmured between sniffles. "I didn't know love could be this way. I didn't know..."

"I don't understand."

"Mom and dad, they're both wonderful apart, but together all they do is fight. That's why I spent so much time at the barn growing up. I couldn't stand being home. Horses are safe. I love them and they love me back."

"Carly..."

"I may have shown you how to trust and love a horse, but you're showing me I can trust and love another person. I mean—trust and love you, and I do. There's no effort. Loving you is as easy as breathing."

"Yeah, as easy as breathin'," he murmured. "How would you feel about gettin' on that plane tonight?"

"I'd drive to the airport with just the clothes on my back right now if I could."

"Fair warnin'. When you get here I'm gonna hug you super tight, and I'm never, ever, lettin' you outta my sight again."

"Promise?"

"You bet your chaps!"

EPILOGUE

Connie Masters bought Domino, and it was a record purchase for Dream Horse Ranch. When Andy had quoted Connie the sales price, he'd expected her to counter with half the amount, but she hadn't batted an eye.

A few days later, the horse whisperer dentist confirmed Carly's suspicions. Preston did have a bad tooth. After a simple procedure, he too was sold for more money than Andy had expected.

A couple of weeks later, early one afternoon, he cleaned himself up, put on his best shirt and jacket, climbed into his truck and drove to the local cafe. Pulling into the parking lot, he'd felt an unfamiliar rush of nerves, but taking a deep breath, he walked into the quaint dining room. Maureen O'Toole, the beautiful red-headed owner, stood behind the counter. She had lost her husband several years before, and it was only his commitment to Dream Horse Ranch that had prevented Andy from approaching her sooner. As he sat at a table by the window, she walked over, smiled her warm smile, and tilted her head to the side.

"Andy, you're looking spiffy today. Special occasion?"

"Uh, yeah, I guess you could say that," he'd managed, trying to find his normally unruffled self who had evidently taken the day off. "I'm here to ask if you'd like to come out to Dream Horse Ranch for dinner tomorrow night, or any night, or lunch, but I'm sure you're busy at lunch, probably dinner time too. Whatever suits you."

Feeling like a complete idiot, he couldn't believe it when she pulled out a chair and sat down opposite him.

"Andy, I'd be delighted. I can come any time."

"You can? What about this place?"

"I have someone who can cover me."

"Great, then, uh, you tell me when it suits you."

"Tomorrow night would be fine," she'd said softly, then with a twin-kle in her bright blue eyes, she added, "It sure took you a while to get around to this. Let me guess, is it a long story?"

Suddenly finding his feet, he smiled broadly and wrapped his fingers around her soft feminine hand.

"Yeah, Maureen, you could call it that."

* * *

Theresa Cavalleri had been easy to find. Working as a waitress in a diner on the outskirts of Houston, and living in a small studio apartment, she opened her door early one evening to find her long-lost, little brother standing in front of her.

"Am I dreaming?" she sputtered, then tears springing from her eyes, she threw her arms around him. "I can't believe it. Sal, my little Sal."

Shortly after their reunion, Heath invited her to visit for a few days. Refusing to take no for an answer, he booked her a flight, and he and Salvo drove to the airport to pick her up.

Theresa had never been out of the city. She fell in love with the open space, and though initially nervous, she adored the horses. Heath found her to be a female version of her brother. Good-natured, slightly reserved, and when she asked if she could help around the barn, she was just as enthusiastic and hard-working.

* * *

Carly's father represented Gary Campbell at his parole hearing and came out victorious, but after the apprehension of Brice Connor, the truth came out, and Gary's conviction was overturned. Elsie was in Houston restoring her relationship with Harlan when Gary was released. Their reunion had been filled with joyful tears, and she'd returned to the ranch with Gary in tow.

With Elsie wanting to spend more time with the man she loved and had missed so much, Heath approached Theresa and asked if she'd be interested in stepping in to pick up the slack. Theresa was thrilled, and introduced her special brand of Italian cooking.

The temporary arrangement worked out so well, when Elsie wanted to return to Houston to spend more time with Harlan, and Gary needed to go back to sort out his business affairs, Heath hired Theresa to replace her.

The ranch would be Elsie's second home, and her apartment would remain untouched, but Theresa was offered the cabin, or a room in the house. She gleefully accepted the cabin.

* * *

During the long weeks of Harlan's recovery, Mitzi had shown her true character. She'd stayed at his side every day, brought him gifts, books to read, and whatever else she could think of to keep his spirits up. When he finally returned home, she prepared a special dinner, and Heath, Carly, Elsie and Gary were there to welcome him. Though thinner, his warm, jovial personality had returned, and over dessert, he rose to his feet.

"We've all suffered at the hands of Brice Connor, but now he's the one behind bars, and we're back together, and Gary is an executive at Boyd Holdings. Who would have seen that coming? Mitzi, my beautiful lady, you have been a constant source of comfort. How you put up with me while I was spaced out I don't know. You're an angel," he said gratefully, then took a deep, dramatic breath. "Heath, you know I loved your mother very much," he continued, "and I still love her. I also know she wants my life to be complete, so, uh, Mitzi, will you do me the honor of becoming the second Mrs. Harlan Boyd?"

Her happy tears freely flowing, she jumped to her feet, hugged Harlan and fervently blubbered her acceptance.

Watching the joyous moment, a sudden wave of heat moved through Heath's body.

The same heat he'd experienced the night he'd been standing at the kitchen door and experienced the remarkable epiphany about his life.

Touching the key beneath his shirt, as if struck by a bolt of lightning, he knew it was time to make his relationship with Carly permanent.

A moment later, he flashed back to earlier in the day.

He'd had an inspired thought about a gift for her. Carly had been on her way to do some shopping. He'd joined her, then slipped away and purchased the special gift.

Had it been a coincidence?

* * *

The following day was warm and sunny. Mitzi and Harlan had left to enjoy lunch at Harlan's favorite restaurant, while Carly and Heath enjoyed the unseasonably warm weather in the pool. They'd been playing in the water, and as they climbed out and settled into deck chairs, Heath was about to reach for the gift, when a panicked chill rippled through him. The chain around his neck was gone.

"No, no, no," he exclaimed, jumping to his feet and darting his eyes across the ground. "Where the hell is it?"

"Where's what?" Carly asked anxiously. "Heath? What have you lost?"

"My chain and key."

"Oh, no," she exclaimed, staring up at him wide-eyed. "Heath, stop for a second. I'm sure it was around your neck when we were in the pool. Yes, it was, I remember."

"You do?" he said urgently, running to the side of the pool and peering into the water. "Thank God. There it is!"

He dove in the water, reappearing with it clutched in his fist a moment later. Climbing out and sitting on the edge of the chair, he discovered the chain had broken.

"Dammit. I wonder how that happened."

"Heath," Carly said softly, handing him a black box wrapped with a gold bow. "I had this made for you. I said I wanted to go shopping, but really I just needed to pick it up."

"Really? Thank you. I have something for you as well."

"You do? That's a coincidence."

"I'm beginning to think there's no such thing."

Untying the ribbon and lifting out the black velvet box, he opened it up.

His heart skipped.

A silver key hung from a silver heart on a long chain.

Tucked into the lid sat a hand written card.

I have only one heart, it has only one key, and they both belong to you.

"That's engraved on the back," she said quietly, "and that's not silver. I chose white gold. I thought regular gold would be too garish, and I, uh, I thought perhaps you could wear it next to the one your mother gave you."

Staring at it, a hot lump sprang to life in his throat, then he looked back at the broken chain on the table.

"Carly, this is...sorry, I have no words, but we don't need them."

Almost overwhelmed with the heavy emotion sweeping through his soul, he placed it around his neck, then contemplating the gift his mother had given him so long ago, he broke into a smile.

"I know exactly what to do. Have both photographs of the ranch mounted in one frame, and my mother's chain and key above them."

"Heath—that's perfect."

"That's where it belongs now. That's my history, and this," he said, holding the heart and key she'd just given him, "just like you, this is my present and my future. I'll treasure it forever."

"I'm so glad you love it. To be honest, considering your mother's chain just broke, I'm beginning to wonder if it was even my idea."

They both laughed, and taking her hand he brought her to her feet and wrapped her up in his arms.

"We're pure magic," he purred. "It's been one miracle after another."

"Especially surviving the branch plowing through my windshield."

"Especially that," he murmured. "Now, my beautiful girl, you have to open the gift I bought for you."

Breaking their hug, he reached for the box he'd hidden under a towel.

"Our love is timeless," he said as he handed it to her. "Carly, I wanna be with you forever."

Swallowing back her happy tears, she opened the box. A gold Rolex watch with a white face and diamonds stared up at her.

"Heath, this is absolutely gorgeous. I can't believe you bought me a Rolex. I'll be afraid to wear it."

"Tomorrow I wanna take you to a private jeweler so you can pick out a ring," he said softly, lifting it out and placing it around her wrist, "or you can design your own if you want. He's here in Houston. I've made an appointment with him tomorrow afternoon. Carly Kincaid, will you marry me?"

"I'll, uh, need some time," she said solemnly, dropping her eyes, then lifting them, she grinned up at him. "Okay, yes."

"You just gave me a frickin' heart attack. I'm gonna spank you so dang hard."

"Really? YAY. It worked!"

* * *

A local photographer crafted a uniquely hinged case for the two photographs and the precious chain and key, leaving room to accommodate more mementos as life on the ranch evolved. The chain was above the pictures just as Heath had envisioned, in a horizontal line with the key on a holder in the center to keep it straight. With Carly and Heath looking on, the talented artist had mounted it in Heath's office.

The wedding ceremony took place at the ranch, but Harlan insisted on a big party two days later at his home. They agreed, but left early to catch a flight to New Zealand for their honeymoon. It was a fabulous and fascinating two weeks. They stayed at a quaint bed and breakfast on a sheep farm, rode horses over rolling green hills, and hiked through tropical forests, but the time in the picturesque land flew by too fast.

It was late in the evening when they rolled up to the gates of Dream Horse Ranch. Both tired from the long flight, Heath had called ahead and asked Andy to hold off on any welcome home celebrations until the following day. When they walked in they were grateful to find it quiet and empty.

"Let's leave the unpacking until the morning?" Carly said wearily as they entered the bedroom. "I can't deal with it. I just want to take a shower and crawl into bed."

"Sounds good to me," Heath replied, placing their suitcases by the closet. "I'll get the rest of the bags then as well. I just wanna stop in the office real quick."

As he walked away, Carly began to peel off her clothes, but it was only a minute later he was urgently calling her. Moving swiftly from the room and down the hall she raced in to join him.

"Heath? What's the matter?"

"Look."

He was pointing at the newly mounted photographs. Gazing up at the case, she caught her breath. The key had come off its bracket and the chain was no longer in a straight line, but an arc.

"Oh, my gosh," Carly exclaimed. "Heath, do you see what that is?"

"A smile," he beamed, putting his arm around her, "the biggest smile I've ever seen."

THE END

Dear Reader:

Thank you for buying this book. If you have a moment I would greatly appreciate your review. I constantly strive to bring you interesting and enjoyable content and your feedback is valued. Feel free to contact me at any time. I love to hear from readers. My email is: MagCarpenter@yahoo.com, and here are my social media links should you care to check them out.

My very best wishes,

Maggie

http://www.MaggieCarpenter.com

https://www.facebook.com/MaggieCarpenterWriter

https://twitter.com/magcarpenter2

Copyright © 2017 Maggie Carpenter

All rights reserved. Except as permitted under the U.S. Copyright Act of 1976, no part of this publication may be reproduced, distributed, or transmitted in any form or by any means, or stored in a database or retrieval system, without prior written permission of the publisher.

This book is a work of fiction. The characters, incidents, and dialogue are drawn from the author's imagination and are not to be construed as real. Any resemblance to actual events or persons, living or dead is coincidental.

BOOKS BY MAGGIE CARPENTER

#1 Bestseller:
ROUGH COWBOY
HUNKS and HORSES
A FOUR BOOK SERIES - HEA - STANDALONE
(Featuring characters from COWBOY: His Ranch. His Rules. His Secrets)
TO KISS A COWBOY
TO CATCH A COWBOY
TO CON A COWBOY
TO TRUST A COWBOY
SEXY SCIFI - PARANORMAL
ROUGH ALPHA
TRAINED BY THE ALIEN
WARLOCK
THE ALIEN'S RULES
BDSM CONTEMPORARY ROMANCE
ROUGH ROAD
ROUGH ROCKSTAR
THE STRICT BRITISH BARRISTER: BOOKS 1 & 2
SINS BEHIND THE SCENES
I AM A DOMINANT
DESIRE UNLEASHED - Sexsomnia
TIMELESS OBSESSION
For a full list of her novels visit her author page.
https://www.amazon.com/author/maggiecarpente

Printed in Great Britain
by Amazon

61107735R00116